TROUBLE BREWING

ANNA MARKLAND

OLIVERHEART BOOKS

Dedicated to my Lancashire ancestors.

"We live as long as we're remembered."

Author's Note

As an amateur genealogist (aka an addict of family tree research) I became obsessed with tracing my English roots back to the Norman Conquest in the 11th century.

This turned out to be a pipe dream since I am not descended from the nobility and records were not kept for "common folks" until much later. Even then, early parish records are often indecipherable.

As a result, I began to write stories about a noble medieval family I conjured from my imagination. The Montbryce family was born.

Like many people, I had an inner compulsion to write one good book. What was originally intended as that one book about my fictional family eventually became the 12-book series, The Montbryce Legacy.

In other words, writing superseded genealogy as my principal addiction, and I have since published more than 60 novels and novellas. Almost all are historical romances that feature Vikings, Highlanders, medieval knights, Elizabethan goldsmiths, Regency aristocrats or Victorian industrialists. You can find more details on my website https://annamarkland.com/.

I've lived most of my life in Canada, though I was born in the UK. An English grammar school education instilled in me a love of European history which continues to this day. While I may boast of being a proud Canadian, I'm still a Lancashire lass at heart.

Before becoming a full-time writer, I was an elementary school teacher, a job I loved. I then worked as administrator for a world-wide disaster relief organization.

I love cats, although I haven't been able to bring myself to adopt another one since unexpectedly losing Topaz a few years ago.

I have few domestic skills. You'll notice most of my heroines hate sewing!

I try to follow three simple writing guidelines. I give my characters free rein to tell their story, which often turns out to be different from the original version in my head. I'm a firm believer in love at first sight. My protagonists may initially deny the attraction but, eventually, my heroes and heroines find their soul mates. It seems only natural then to include scenes of intimacy enjoyed by people who love each other deeply. I believe such intimacy is wholesome. Historical accuracy is important to me, although I have been known to tweak history when necessary. I write romance because I find happy endings very satisfying.

You can find me on all the usual social media platforms. On Facebook as Anna Markland and Anna Markland Novels, on Instagram as annamarkland, on X as @annamarkland, and Pinterest and BookBub as Anna Markland. I also have a reader group on Facebook called Markland's Merrymakers and new members are always welcome.

I'd like to acknowledge the invaluable contributions of my beta readers, Maria McIntyre and Alison Pridie.

Chapter 1

Drowning In Beer

Bolton, Lancashire, 1862

"At least 'e died 'appy," the brewmaster chortled.

Gathered around the mash tun, curious brewery workers chuckled their general agreement with Jenkinson's witty comment.

Unreasonably out of breath after climbing the ladder up to the platform in a panic, Jacob didn't see anything funny in a boiled corpse floating in the mash tun of his brewery. "He doesn't look very happy to me," he gasped. "Who is he?"

"Damned if I know," Jenkinson replied. "'E were face down, but we turned 'im o'er wi' a paddle. None of us recognize 'im."

Jacob wasn't surprised. The hot water had blistered the dead man's face. "This'll cost us time we can't afford to lose, not to mention the wasted malt. Fish him out, then drain the tun."

"We'd best wait 'til the poleece come," Jenkinson said with great solemnity.

"You sent for the police?" Jacob demanded. "Just because some idiot fell into the mash tun?"

"Well, aye," Jenkinson replied. "I don't think 'e fell. There's a ruddy great 'ole int back of 'is 'ead."

Voices below in the brewery entrance heralded the arrival of two policemen, one of whom was the tallest man Jacob had ever seen. By the time they'd climbed the wooden ladder up to the raised platform, the giant was more out of breath than Jacob.

"Inspector Marcus Halliwell," he panted, making no effort to extend his hand as he clutched the railing. "And this is Constable Walsh. What have we here then?"

"I'm Jacob Longworth," Jacob began.

"You own Longworth's Brewery, I assume," the Constable said, scribbling in a notebook after licking the lead of his pencil.

The Inspector scowled, apparently as irritated as Jacob by the interruption.

"Yes," Jacob replied. "Jenkinson here found the body. He's the brewmaster, so I'll let him explain."

Halliwell listened closely to Jenkinson's account, then appeared to speak to the corpse that was by now floating face down again. Walsh made a note of everything Jenkinson said, but pointedly ignored his mumbling superior.

"Let's get him out then," the Inspector finally said.

The workers used hooks to drag the body over the side of the tun so as not to scald their hands.

"Well dressed, whoever he is," the Constable remarked, as the corpse landed on the platform with a watery thud.

"Blimey," Jenkinson exclaimed. "I recognize the fancy waistcoat now. It's Mr. Longworth's chum, Mr. Sharp."

Jacob's throat constricted. Richard Sharp had recently bought up his IOUs and had become a frequent visitor to the brewery, but he was certainly no friend of Jacob's. "You may be right," he allowed, relieved the extortionist was dead, but worried suspicion was likely to fall on him.

Halliwell searched the dead man's pockets. "Nothing on him except a sodden cigar and a soaking wet calling card," he told them, holding the items in his palm.

Jacob clenched his jaw. It was imperative he lay his hands

on the proof of his debts. Assuming Sharp had heirs, there was no guarantee they wouldn't in turn threaten his ownership of the brewery.

Strident female voices raised in song drew everyone's attention to the yard outside. "Temperance League fanatics," he hissed. "Today of all days."

Gratified by the large number of women from the Temperance League who'd turned out for the protest outside Longworth's Brewery, Lady Jane Yate pressed the loud-hailer to her lips. "Raise your voices, ladies, and leave no doubt in their minds that we mean business." Clearing her dry throat, Jane hoped to hit the right note to start off the rallying cry. This was one aspect of spearheading a protest that she dreaded. In her aristocratic mother's opinion, a suitable husband would never pursue a woman who couldn't carry a tune. Any nobleman worth his salt needed a wife who could entertain at musicales.

Raise the banner high, let it wave from sea to sea, Jane sang, painfully aware she was off-key.

Aware of her musical shortcomings, her stalwart followers took up the song.

> *For temperance's cause, we stand in unity.*
> *With faith and hope unfaltering, we strive to*
>   *make it right,*
> *Together we are stronger, marching for the light.*

Relieved her followers had carried the day and made up for her embarrassing failure to start them off on the right note, she sang the verse with them.

*Taverns and alehouses must close their doors at
    last,
For in their shadows, our dreams and joys have
    passed.
No more shall the demon drink drown our future
    bright,
We seek a world of virtue, where temperance is
    the right.*

THE ENTHUSIASTIC VOICES trailed off and nervous chatter began when two men emerged from the brewery. The uniformed policeman stood at least six feet tall. Longworth had apparently called the law. The protest wasn't illegal, but Jane braced herself for censure.

"Excuse me, ma'am," the giant said, removing his stovepipe hat. "May I know your name?"

"Lady Jane Yate," she replied, squaring her shoulders and wishing she hadn't been born the runt of her parents' extensive litter as she craned her neck to look up. "We have every right..."

"I'm Inspector Halliwell, Your Ladyship. Perhaps I should make you aware there has been a death at Mr. Longworth's brewery, so..."

Prepared for a confrontation, Jane was stunned by the revelation. As he carried on explaining that a man had been found floating in a vat of beer, she was rendered speechless—a rarity for a woman who prided herself on her outspokenness. It came to her that the second man was none other than Jacob Longworth—arch-enemy of the Women's Temperance League. Instead of the portly, aging industrialist she'd expected, she found herself looking into the concerned blue eyes of a beautiful, broad-shouldered man with sandy hair who couldn't be a day over twenty-five. He wasn't as tall as the giant policeman, but he towered over Jane as he took her hand and bestowed a courtly kiss. "I would appreciate it if you could hold your protest some other day, Lady Jane."

His mode of speech and his gentlemanly gesture bespoke an educated man of good breeding. Annoyingly flummoxed, Jane gaped, stupidly wondering if he cared whether a woman could sing or not.

Jacob had heard a great deal of talk about Lady Jane Yate and her Temperance League. In his mind's eye, he'd imagined a middle-aged harridan, probably pock-faced. The petite spitfire leading the charge outside his brewery took him by surprise and had an unsettling effect on parts of his male body he normally kept under strict control. A man didn't succeed in the cutthroat business of brewing beer by running after every female that came along, especially one reportedly determined to shut down his brewery. Perhaps it was the red hair, or the wide, green eyes that had his balls in an uproar? Or was it the whiff of lavender when he kissed her dainty hand? He'd always been a sucker for lavender.

Returning to the brewery with the policeman, he forced his mind away from intoxicating perfume and bewitching green eyes back to the grisly matter at hand. "I should tell you," he began, as he ushered Halliwell into his cramped office. "I do know the deceased, although, contrary to what Jenkinson said, Richard Sharp was no friend of mine."

"Sounds like you didn't like him much," the Constable remarked as he joined them.

Jacob dithered, wondering how much of his association with

Sharp he should reveal. "No, I didn't. He was trying to extort money from me."

The Constable eyed him suspiciously before scribbling in his notebook. Jacob should perhaps have kept that piece of information to himself. He now appeared to have a motive for killing Sharp.

"Care to explain?" Halliwell asked.

"He recently bought up several of my IOUs and was using them to threaten me."

"IOUs?"

Jacob fervently wished he hadn't revealed any of this unsavory business. "Three years ago, I borrowed extensively to open this brewery. My creditors agreed to allow me to pay them off over time. It seems Sharp made them an offer they couldn't refuse."

"And what was he threatening to do?"

"Take control of the brewery if I didn't pay him in full within the week."

He had a sinking feeling he had just sealed his fate.

Chapter 2

The Investigation Begins

The arrival of Sydney Spilsbury necessitated curtailing the interview with Longworth. Marcus introduced the pathologist to the brewery owner, then led the way up the rickety ladder. Someone had covered the body with a cloth, which Spilsbury hastily removed and tossed to the floor below. "Contamination," he muttered petulantly.

Too busy worrying about the reason he found climbing ladders increasingly difficult these days, Marcus paid scant attention. At the age of thirty, he should still be fit as a fiddle, but he acknowledged he'd let himself go after his beloved Eliza's death. If he didn't do something about his health, his young constable would quickly surpass him in rank. Walsh had already ingratiated himself with the incompetent Superintendent by sharing information Marcus had gathered about the murder at *The Hippodrome Music Hall.* Walsh was convinced they'd arrested and charged the guilty party—Edouard Deschanel, proprietor of the *Shangri-La* luxury goods store—but Marcus wasn't so sure. The constable had yet to learn the importance of loyalty to his inspector. Marcus could never fully trust his assistant until he did.

"Help me turn him over, Constable," Spilsbury said.

Marcus was thankful Walsh was present to aid the patholo-gist. Heights made him dizzy and he was reluctant to let go of the railing. He hoped the ambitious constable hadn't noticed, but Walsh didn't miss much.

"A hammer, most likely," Spilsbury declared after exam-ining the wound on the back of the victim's head. "I'll send men from the mortuary to remove the body. No one else is to touch him."

They turned Sharp onto his back before descending to the floor below. "This area will be out of bounds for the foreseeable future," Spilsbury told Longworth who was waiting at the bottom of the ladder.

"But I need to drain the mash tun and clean it out," Long-worth exclaimed. "I can't afford to have the brewery sit idle."

Spilsbury shrugged and walked away, leaving Longworth fuming.

Retreating to his office, Jacob's mind filled with a hundred ways to distract the constable from watching over the corpse—all of them impractical. However, he had to make sure the IOUs weren't in some hidden pocket. Sharp was devious.

In the meantime, he had practical matters to take care of. There was beer in the kettles and the fermentation vat, but the entire process would grind to a halt if the mash tun was still out of bounds once that supply had been bottled or barreled.

Jenkinson and his helpers were loyal workers who'd been with him since the beginning, but he'd have to lay them off if it came to shutting down the whole operation. Jenkinson would soon find work with another brewery. He'd be a great loss. The man had a flair when it came to creating new types of ale. It was ironic. In death, Sharp may have accomplished what Lady Jane Yate desired most.

He sat up straight when the constable suddenly stretched and started down the ladder. If he was answering the call of nature, Jacob might have a couple of minutes to...

Already halfway out of his chair, he slumped back down when Walsh greeted two men in brown warehouse coats. Five minutes later, the body had been carried down the ladder and loaded into a hearse.

Frustrated, Jacob realized he would have to devise some other way of getting his hands on the vowels.

THE CALLING card found in the dead man's pocket had eventually dried. Though it was discolored, enough of the owner's name was still visible to bring Marcus and Walsh to a large house in Heaton, one of Bolton's better neighborhoods. Marcus stood back and allowed Walsh to lift the knocker of the opulent mansion's front door.

"We'd like to speak to Lord Jonas Sperling," Walsh informed the gaunt butler who answered the door.

Comical wisps of fine gray hair standing on end put Marcus in mind of a dandelion clock. He wished he hadn't thought of that when he remembered Eliza's delight in blowing the seeds off dandelion heads. Sometimes he wondered if he would ever get over her loss, or would little things always remind him of her?

He banished the painful memory when the butler returned after rudely leaving them standing on the front step. "I'm afraid his lordship is entertaining visitors at the moment and cannot be disturbed."

Marcus thrust the card under the butler's nose before he

could slam the heavy door. "Please inform your master we found his calling card in the pocket of a murder victim. It's imperative we speak with him as soon as possible."

Walsh elbowed his way into the foyer before the old fellow could object. Marcus had to concede his constable's rough-and-ready ways sometimes came in useful.

Leaving them to cool their heels in the foyer, the butler disappeared, emerging a few moments later with the news his lordship would receive them in the drawing room.

"Inspector Halliwell," Marcus informed the two young men they encountered lounging on a settee in the drawing room. He doffed his stovepipe, tucked it under his arm, and introduced his constable.

"I'm Sperling. What's this about?" the taller of the two gents demanded.

"You might prefer we discuss this matter in private," Marcus replied.

"No need," Sperling replied nasally. "Lord Francis Yate and I are bosom beaux."

Sperling's bosom beau could be Lady Jane's brother, but the glass of spirits in his hand indicated he wasn't supportive of his sister's involvement with the Temperance movement. Marcus deemed it wiser not to make mention of her presence at the brewery. "As you wish. This morning we attended the scene of a murder. The body of Mr. Richard Sharp was discovered at Longworth's brewery."

"Good grief," Yate exclaimed, spilling some of his liquor as he struggled to extricate himself from the settee. "You're sure it was Sharp?"

"Steady on, old thing," Sperling advised, glaring at his friend. "You say this chap had my calling card in his possession?"

"Yes. Do you know how he came to have it?"

"No idea," Sperling replied. "I hand them out willy-nilly. Who knows where they turn up?"

"So, you didn't know Richard Sharp?"

"Not remotely," Sperling asserted.

His chum's outburst and subsequent pallor made Marcus suspect Sperling was lying. However, he had no choice but to take his leave. "Thank you, my lords. Forgive the intrusion."

As soon as he and the constable were shown out by the butler, Walsh said, "They're lying. They both knew him."

"Well spotted," Marcus replied. "I think you may be right, but which one seemed more shocked by the news?"

"Yate," Walsh replied. "Do you suppose he's related to Lady Jane Yate?"

STILL CONFUSED AND embarrassed by her body's disturbing physical reaction to Jacob Longworth, Jane hurried home after consulting briefly with her followers. In Glenairlie's foyer, she handed her gloves and hat to Nelthorpe. "Is Papa home?" she asked the elderly butler, though there really was no need. Her father's commanding voice echoed despite the fact his study was at the far end of a long hallway.

"In his study with Lord Francis," Nelthorpe replied, as he assisted her to remove her woolen cloak.

Jane prayed for patience. She loved her father and brother but could never reveal they were the principal reason she had joined the Women's Temperance League. Both men drank to excess, excusing their obvious addiction as something that was expected of members of the nobility. In her opinion, this argument didn't hold water. Her eldest brother, George, Viscount Burnley, drank wine with his meals and enjoyed the occasional glass of brandy. That was the extent of his drinking. Jane was the youngest child of seven and the only girl. Francis was the one sibling who seemed to have inherited their father's tendency to over-imbibe.

Judging by the increasingly loud argument going on in the study, Jane assumed both men were well on their way to inebriation. Then she caught the word *murder*.

She couldn't reveal that she'd been present at the brewery, but curiosity got the better of her. She tapped on the door of the study and entered without waiting for permission.

Both men glared at her like little boys caught in the act of mischief-making.

"Forgive the intrusion, Papa," she crooned, knowing from experience he would forgive his only daughter any transgression. "Did I hear you say someone had been murdered?"

"Er..." Francis mumbled.

"Such matters aren't for the ears of delicate young ladies," her father grunted. "However, you may as well be told that Richard Sharp has been murdered at a local brewery."

Upon hearing the news that a man she despised was dead and that she'd unwittingly been present at the selfsame brewery, Jane surrendered to overwhelming relief and fainted.

Chapter 3

The Same Page

B ack at the central Bolton Borough police station, Marcus approached his superintendent. "What do we know about the Yate family?" he asked.

He had scant respect for his superior, who tended to jump to conclusions instead of relying on sound police work, but it was well known the man hobnobbed with the upper classes.

"The Earl of Leyland's brood?"

Marcus nodded, hoping he wasn't going to regret poking into the lives of a noble family.

"The Earl is a bit too fond of his liquor, but he's a good sort. Wife's something of a harridan. Seven children, all boys, except for the youngest."

"Lady Jane."

"Yes, apparently an agitator in the Temperance movement, I hear."

"I met her this morning. She was leading a protest at the brewery."

"The place where the murder took place?"

"Yes, then, in the course of our inquiries, I encountered her brother at the home of Lord Jonas Sperling."

"Which brother?"

"Francis."

"The black sheep of the family."

"He and Sperling denied knowing Sharp, though Sperling's calling card was found in the victim's pocket. Yate didn't admit it, but his reaction showed he definitely knew the victim."

"Guilty then."

Even Walsh rolled his eyes.

"We don't believe he is the killer, sir."

His superior mumbled something under his breath, then asked, "Do we know anything about the dead man?"

"The brewery owner claims Sharp was trying to extort money from him."

"There's your motive then. Arrest him."

Marcus reminded himself that patience was a virtue, even in the face of a superior who always jumped to erroneous conclusions. "It could be that Sharp was extorting money from other people besides Longworth."

The superintendent steepled his hands while he considered this possibility. A sudden deep frown indicated he realized what Marcus was getting at. "Surely you don't mean the Yate family? Tread carefully, Halliwell. We mustn't alienate the nobility."

As he left the office, Marcus wondered what Walsh would make of being careful not to offend members of the nobility. His young constable had previously made no secret of his disdain for anyone with wealth.

JANE WRINKLED HER NOSE, coughing as the pungent odor of smelling salts stole up her nostrils.

"There she be," Florrie exclaimed with great satisfaction.

Jane pushed away the disgusting vial. "What happened?"

she asked the Scottish maid who'd served the family for years. Florrie was more of a mother to her than the countess.

"Ye fainted," Florrie replied. "Lord Francis carried ye upstairs."

Fainted? Lady Jane Yate never fainted. She was made of sterner stuff. The news Richard Sharp, the persistent philanderer, was dead had come as a big relief.

Hearing the crunch of carriage wheels on the gravel driveway below her window, Jane struggled to sit up in the big bed. "What's happening?"

"That'll be young Frederick, I 'spect, and his da."

"My uncle and cousin?" Jane asked, repulsed by mention of her odious relatives. "What are they doing here?"

"Blowed if I ken. Yer father's called a family meeting, a gatherin' o' the clan."

"Without me?" Jane exclaimed, leaping out of bed. "Fetch my shoes."

Ten minutes later, still furious that her uncle and cousin had been notified of the meeting and she hadn't, she hurried downstairs and burst into her father's study. The initial shock on the faces of her male siblings was soon replaced by an amused acceptance of their little sister's tendency to cause a stir by appearing in a disheveled state in polite company. Only her eldest brother, George, smiled a welcome. Eliot wrinkled his nose as if detecting a bad smell. Francis, Victor, Albert, and Edward all rolled their eyes. "Monkey see, monkey do," she murmured to herself.

"Jane," her frowning father growled.

"Papa," she replied sweetly, wishing she'd taken the time to see to her toilette as she chose a seat next to George—as far away from the grinning Frederick as possible. If her dear father knew the liberties her oily cousin had taken in trying to force her into marriage, she was certain he wouldn't have been invited to this family summit.

If she revealed anything of his inappropriate behavior to her father, his own twin brother would stoutly deny it and accuse her of lying. Uncle Clarence thought his only son could do no wrong.

As she squeezed in next to him on the settee, George made room and put a brotherly arm around her shoulder. Despite being the heir to their father's earldom, her eldest brother had always protected her. She felt safe with him, but worried what he might do if he knew about Frederick's unseemly advances. George was a master swordsman and a crack shot, but things could go terribly wrong in a duel. Dueling was illegal and she wouldn't put it past Frederick to cheat. A duel with a relative would be scandalous. Frederick had vaguely threatened to ruin her father and to spread the rumor she was a woman of loose morals who'd tried to seduce him. She dismissed the threat to herself as impossible to prove, but the threat to her father was worrisome. She wondered what Frederick could possibly do to ruin her dear Papa—his own uncle.

"So," her father declared, dragging her wandering thoughts back to the reason for the gathering. "Richard Sharp has been murdered."

"What?" Uncle Clarence gasped.

"I don't know who that ith," Frederick declared.

Jane rolled her eyes. She often thought her despicable cousin had adopted the habit of lisping and pronouncing his r's as w's in the belief it was expected of a young nobleman. Her uncle clearly knew Sharp and must have known the reason for the summons to Glenairlie. "Drowned in a vat of ale," she supplied, unable to resist baiting the pair.

"How do you know this?" Papa asked.

Her throat constricted. Assuming Sharp was the victim of

the murder at the brewery, she'd spoken without forethought—as usual. "Er...Florrie told me," she fibbed. "Servants hear news of such things long before we do."

Papa squared his shoulders. "Well, the police have already spoken to Francis, so we must all be on the same page if and when we are questioned."

"The same page?" George asked.

"This family cannot be implicated. No member of the Yate family left the house during the time the murder was committed, and we will make no mention of Sharp's attempts to extort money from members of this family or anyone of our acquaintance."

"Extorthion?" Frederick exclaimed. "I mutht confess to knowing nothing of thuch matters."

"Nor I," Uncle Clarence echoed.

An icy chill raced up and down Jane's spine. Sharp was afflicted with the same wandering-hands problem as Frederick, and she suspected he too had been holding something incriminating over her father's head. Her uncle and cousin claimed not to know Sharp, but she'd learned from experience not to trust a word they said.

She sensed undercurrents swirling in the room. Even George seemed ill-at-ease.

Chapter 4

Lie Upon Lie

Over the course of the following week, Jacob's frustration grew as he watched investigators swarm up and down the ladder to the mash tun. They spent hours examining the platform—a futile exercise in his opinion. What were they hoping to find? Meanwhile, the contaminated mash continued to deteriorate. The reek was becoming intolerable, not to mention the flies. If this went on much longer, he'd be obliged to have a new mash tun made—an expense he could ill afford, not to mention the delay. He was already behind with some orders. Publicans became impatient and took their custom elsewhere if he didn't deliver on time. Despite the brewery staff's efforts to quell news of the murder, several orders had been cancelled.

He sensed unease among his workforce. A gruesome murder was enough to unsettle even the bravest heart, but, for the casual laborers, the threat of unemployment loomed like a rock on which their families would founder, especially at a time when most of the local cotton mills sat idle because of the cotton famine.

Finally, Inspector Halliwell turned up and let him know the area was no longer out of bounds. "Did your team find whatever they were looking for?" Jacob asked, more out of exasperation than a wish to know.

"Depends," Halliwell replied.

Jacob's gut told him to leave well alone, but he couldn't resist. "On what?" he asked.

Halliwell tapped the side of his nose in reply which only served to exasperate Jacob further.

"I take it we can now clean out the mash tun?" he asked.

"You can."

Gathered around them, Jenkinson and his men breathed a collective sigh of relief and were soon scrambling up the ladder to begin the unpleasant task.

As he was about to leave, Halliwell turned back. "One more thing, Mr. Longworth—do you know Lord Jonas Sperling?"

Jacob was tempted to laugh. "I'm a tradesman," he replied. "Members of the upper class do not socialize with the likes of me."

"How about Lord Francis Yate?"

Jacob hesitated, taken aback by the question. Was this Lord Francis Yate related to the petite firebrand he couldn't get out of his mind? "No," he finally replied, though he realized from Halliwell's frown he'd taken too long to answer. "I was simply wondering..."

He stopped himself just in time. It would be foolhardy to show any interest in a woman bent on destroying him.

"He's Lady Jane's brother," Halliwell said, smiling as he took his leave.

For the following fortnight, Marcus had scant opportunity to deal with the murder at the brewery. Thanks to ill-informed decisions made by his superior officer, a man

Marcus believed to be innocent of a murder committed at *The Hippodrome* music hall had been sentenced to be hanged after a farcical trial at the Manchester Assizes. He felt it his duty to continue that investigation despite his superintendent's orders to the contrary.

Proof of the real killer's identity finally came to light and the innocent man freed. It gladdened his heart that Edouard Deschanel and Maggie Chadwick could now marry. His own love story had come to a tragic end with Eliza's untimely death, but he was delighted to see genuine lovers reunited. Unless he missed his guess, young Jacob Longworth was quite taken with Lady Jane Yate. That thought gave him pause. He hoped Longworth wouldn't turn out to be Sharp's murderer.

Free once more to return his attention to the murder at the brewery, he thought back over the two killings he'd managed to solve. In both cases—the beating death of a boy at Broadclough Mills and the garroting of Fred Chadwick at *The Hippodrome*— luck had played as large a part as his investigative talents. Perhaps the same would hold true in this instance and the real killer brought to justice.

Buoyed by renewed optimism after the demotion of his inept superintendent, he and Walsh discussed what they knew already. "According to Longworth, Sharp was into extortion, which means he may have had other enemies besides the brewery owner," Walsh said. "We simply have to uncover their identities and establish means and motive."

Marcus nodded. Perhaps his constable was developing some good instincts. Deschanel's wrongful conviction and subsequent exoneration had apparently made him see the danger in jumping to the wrong conclusions without evidence. "I'd like to question all the members of the Yate family. However, I've mentioned the possibility to the new superintendent and he's advising caution. What he means is we should forget the idea."

Walsh rolled his eyes. "Typical. There must be some way we can interview them."

"Let's at least visit their home and see how things go."

STILL PERTURBED by the puzzling conversation about extortion that had taken place at the family gathering two weeks prior, Jane couldn't concentrate on the book she was reading in the drawing room of Glenairlie. Her thoughts constantly wandered to Jacob Longworth. Equally unsettling was George's unusually agitated behavior.

Her spirits plummeted further when she heard a deep voice from the foyer that she recognized from the brewery the day of the murder. She slammed the book shut, dreading the reason for the tall policeman's visit. His failure to appear for a fortnight had led her to believe the unpleasant matter was resolved.

"What's amiss?" her brother George asked. "You seem agitated."

"No," she lied, contemplating escaping to her room.

She realized she'd dithered too long when her father entered the drawing room, the tall inspector and another policeman with him. Both uniformed visitors had politely removed their stovepipe hats.

"This is my son and heir, Lord George, Viscount Burnley," her father announced to the policemen.

"Marcus Halliwell," the inspector replied, shaking hands with George. "And my assistant, Constable Walsh."

Her father gestured to her. "And my only daughter, Lady Jane."

Jane held her breath, hoping Halliwell would keep her secret.

"Lady Jane," the dear man acknowledged with a polite bow.

"Inspector," she replied with a grateful smile.

"What's this about?" George asked.

"Just routine enquiries, my lord," Halliwell replied. "We're investigating the suspicious death of Mr. Richard Sharp. His body was found floating in the mash tun at Longworth's brewery. It's our understanding your son, Francis, and his friend, Lord Jonas Sperling, were acquainted with him."

"Then perhaps you should speak with them," her father retorted too abruptly for Jane's liking.

"We already did, my lord, but we're wondering if anyone else in the family knew him."

"Not I," George declared.

"Nor I," her father echoed, narrowing his eyes at Jane.

"Nor I," she lied, reluctantly falling into line with her father's expectations.

The policemen politely thanked them for their time and left.

Their father followed them out without a backward glance at his son and daughter.

"No wonder you were nervous," George said unexpectedly. "You were at Longworth's brewery the day of the murder."

"How do you know?" she asked, certain her face had reddened when prickly heat invaded her body.

"I saw you and your marchers there."

It took her a moment to digest what he'd said. "What were you doing at the brewery?" she asked.

"I followed Sharp."

Jane felt like she'd been kicked in the belly. "But you said…"

"I lied, just like the rest of us. But don't worry, I didn't kill him."

Conferring with each other after leaving Glenairlie, Marcus and Walsh agreed the Yates were hiding something. "But how to go about finding out more without offending them?" Marcus mused.

"I don't see why we have to tiptoe around the nobility if they are somehow involved in a crime," Walsh replied.

Marcus sighed. His constable still had a lot to learn. "Thanks to the growing influence of wealthy industrialists, aristocrats may not have the power and prestige they once had here in the north, but they are still a force to be reckoned with. Never assume they're not. A word in the wrong ear could end both our careers in the blink of an eye."

"So, what do you suggest?"

"We need to speak to them individually, without the Earl present. Let's try to question Lord Francis again—by himself this time."

Chapter 5

George's Secret

"We should visit the brewery," George told Jane.

Barely recovered from the shock of his admission that he'd lied, she could only shake her head in response. Discovering her eldest brother wasn't the paragon of virtue she'd assumed was enough to deal with. Although, the prospect of seeing Jacob Longworth again held a tempting appeal she didn't fully comprehend. She hadn't been able to get the handsome man out of her mind.

"I suspect the Inspector is a tenacious fellow who will keep digging until he uncovers the truth," George explained. "If we want to divert attention from this family, we should look into the murder ourselves."

"And how will we do that?"

"You met Longworth and could introduce me to him. Learn what he knows. There must be a reason for Sharp being at the brewery."

Jane almost asked how George had known she'd been introduced to Longworth, but clearly there was more to her brother's involvement with Sharp than she'd even considered. "If I'm to help you, you should be told something about Richard Sharp," she confessed.

"He tried to proposition you," George replied. "It was all I could do not to strangle him when I found out."

"You knew?"

"He told me. Bragged of it in fact."

Jane was afraid to ask for more details.

"Let's just say Sharp knew things about me I'd rather people didn't learn of," he said, as if sensing her confusion.

"He was blackmailing you."

"Exactly. So, are you game to pursue the matter? You're probably the only member of this family I fully trust."

"You mean I'm the only person you believe is innocent of the murder."

"Right again, little sister."

THE BREWERY BECAME a hive of activity as Jenkinson and his crew worked to salvage the mash tun, sterilize it and the platform, and refill the tun with malted grain and hot water. Jacob removed his frock coat, rolled up his sleeves, and pitched in, helping when and where he could. He knew from past experience that working men respected an owner who didn't object to getting his hands dirty.

He regretted his involvement when a gentleman sauntered into the brewery's yard. On his arm came Lady Jane Yate, looking even more deliciously desirable than at their first meeting. They made an interesting pair. The man was tall and muscular. Lady Jane looked like a beautiful miniature doll next to him. They both sported flame-red hair—a brother perhaps. There was something about this petite woman that drew him and sent potent male urges into full throttle. She had the face of an angel and curves in all the right places.

Aware of his inappropriate state of dress, and hoping his arousal wasn't too obvious, he nevertheless hurried down the ladder to greet his visitors.

He hastily rolled down his sleeves when Lady Jane eyed his bare arms. "Forgive me," he said, bestowing a courtly kiss on her knuckles. "It's good to see you again."

He cursed his inane remark. A man had been murdered the last time they'd met—less than ideal circumstances.

"Likewise," she replied. "May I introduce my brother, Lord George Yate, Viscount Burnley."

Jacob's social circle consisted mainly of well-to-do tradesmen like himself. They were successful men, but a world removed from the aristocracy. This man wasn't just an aristocrat, he was the heir to a title. He put paid to Jacob's insecurities by extending a hand, which he accepted. "Viscount," he said, hoping that was the correct form of address. "Jacob Longworth at your service."

Again, he cursed his apparent need to appear subservient.

"George is fine," his visitor replied.

The informality put Jacob on guard. Aristocrats didn't hobnob on a first name basis with people of his class. "How can I help?" he asked, looking straight at Lady Jane. "Not here to plan another protest, I hope."

GEORGE WONDERED if coming to the brewery had been a good idea. Only a fool could fail to notice the spark of attraction between Jane and Longworth. He experienced a pang of pity for his sister. Such a relationship would never be sanctioned by his parents, and George knew only too well what it was to be denied happiness with the person you loved.

Richard Sharp had many faults, some of them criminal in nature, but George had loved him despite the dangers inherent in such a foolish relationship. The sensible and staid George Yate had fallen hard for a ne'er-do-well, a commoner to boot. Blackmail wasn't the problem. A forbidden love was. Perhaps it was as well Richard had been killed. They'd become careless, and if word ever got out that George Yate had unnatural proclivities, his father would disown him.

George rather liked the prospect of inheriting a wealthy earldom, and had no intention of spending his life in prison.

He should caution Jane about becoming involved with Longworth, but what right did he have to tell her whom she could love? He'd yet to pluck up enough courage to share his secret with her, though she was the only sibling he would trust with the truth. However, he was determined to find out who had killed his lover.

"We've come in order to learn more about this man who was murdered," he told the brewer.

Longworth narrowed his eyes. "Richard Sharp? What's your interest in him?"

"I understand my brother Francis was an acquaintance of his, and I simply wanted to make sure..."

"You should speak to the police. I didn't know Sharp and have no idea how he ended up dead in my brewery."

Richard had hinted about his nefarious plans regarding the brewery, so the lie should have come as no surprise. "I believe you didn't kill him, but I am aware he held your vowels, Longworth."

～

JANE'S EMOTIONS were all at sea. While trying desperately to understand what on earth George was talking about, she couldn't get the sight of Jacob Longworth's bare arms out of her head. The golden hair looked soft enough to stroke. Noblemen who bestowed courtly kisses wore gloves. Not only was Jacob not wearing gloves, she felt the roughness of his skin even through her own gloves. It bespoke a man who wasn't afraid of work. He stood in sharp contrast to the idle aristocrats she knew, many of whom were bored with their lives. Jacob obviously lived a busy life. He was real and his vigor intrigued her. Not to mention his moist lips caused unusual pulsing sensations in a very private place. She'd never felt so physically attracted to a man. Her mother would be aghast. Her fellow Temperance League members would think she'd gone over to the enemy.

"Vowels?" she asked, bothered by the stern frown that had replaced Jacob's heart-melting smile.

"IOUs," George explained. "Sharp bought up the brewery's debts. If I'm not mistaken, he was threatening to take over the brewery if Longworth didn't pay up."

"What if he was? That doesn't mean I killed him."

"You don't strike me as a stupid man," George replied. "Killing Richard in your own brewery would be the height of folly and immediately throw suspicion on you."

It didn't escape Jane's notice that George referred to Sharp by his given name. There was too much going on here that she didn't understand, including an inexplicably desperate yearning to establish Jacob's innocence.

George cleared his throat. "Suspicion will fall on anyone who was the victim of Sharp's schemes, including our brother, Francis. I therefore propose we work together to track down the murderer."

❧

Jacob couldn't think straight. Had he not been distracted by Lady Jane's lavender perfume and wide green eyes, he might have been able to deal with her brother's astonishing suggestion.

Yes, the police might suspect him, but there was no evidence to support his involvement. However, it was common knowledge that juries didn't always convict on the basis of evidence. The recent notorious case of Edouard Deschanel was proof of that.

He got the feeling George Yate wasn't forthcoming with the whole truth. He and his sister didn't seem the type to consort with a malicious man like Richard Sharp, yet the viscount had known about the vowels and the threat to the brewery. It was of some consolation that Lady Jane's shocked reaction seemed to indicate she hadn't known. George intimated Sharp may have had other victims. Who were they? Francis Yate, perhaps?

It was imperative Jacob recover his IOUs, but he had no idea where to begin the search. Alone, he had scant hope of success. With Yate's help there might be a chance. The viscount had been on a first name basis with Sharp. Perhaps he held the notes and was simply trying to trick him. If so, why not come right out and tell Jacob he held the notes and expected to be paid? For some unfathomable reason, Yate wanted to track down the killer. The excuse of proving his brother innocent somehow rang hollow.

While Jacob was busy dithering as to what decision to make, Lady Jane laid her delicate gloved hand atop his. "I think we'd make a good team," she said.

He should have rejected the idea, but pleading green eyes filled his beleaguered brain with the arousing prospect of seeing more of her. "I agree," he said.

Chapter 6

More Secrets

Arms folded, Marcus and Walsh lounged beside Lord Francis Yate's carriage outside Sperling's mansion. They didn't have long to wait. When Yate emerged from the house, he noticed them immediately. "If he balks," Marcus said...

"...he's hiding something," Walsh finished.

Yate dithered for a moment, then strolled to his carriage. "Inspector," he said casually, as if policemen waiting by his carriage was an everyday occurrence.

"Lord Francis," Marcus replied. "We'd like to question you further about Richard Sharp."

Frowning, Yate looked around nervously. "Here? In the street where anyone might see us?"

Marcus could imagine how tongues would wag if a lordling were seen being accosted by policemen in the opulent neighborhood. "We can go to the police station, if you prefer. Or we can ride with you and have a private conversation."

"Yes," Yate replied, his frown magically disappearing. "Please, climb aboard."

Marcus settled into his seat, sinking his fingertips into the luxuriously plush squabs.

Walsh sat ramrod straight, notebook and pencil at the ready, his nose clearly out of joint. Marcus resolved to one day get to the bottom of his constable's resentment of the wealthy people with whom they'd come into contact—be they commoners like mill-owner Roger Sandiford, department store magnate Edouard Deschanel, or aristocrats like the Yate family.

Lord Francis took the seat across from Marcus and spent the first few minutes of the journey brushing invisible lint off his trousers. The unmistakable odor of spirits wafted from him, though it was still early in the day. "Well?" he said finally. "What's this about?"

"We want the truth this time," Walsh insisted with a snarl.

"Did you know Richard Sharp?" Marcus asked, anxious to keep the conversation amicable.

After devoting more attention to his trousers, Yate admitted he did know the man. "He was an acquaintance of my father's," he claimed. "And I believe George may have known him."

"Yet both denied it," Marcus said.

"Sharp wasn't the kind of man one admits to knowing. I'm fairly certain he tried to proposition my sister."

Marcus tweaked his mustache. He now had three new suspects to consider. "What about you and Sperling?"

"He was blackmailing us."

The field of possibilities had widened to five. "What was he threatening to reveal?" he asked, as the carriage came to a halt in the driveway of Glenairlie.

"I'd rather not say."

Marcus bristled when Walsh clenched his jaw and fisted his hands. The constable had demonstrated violent tendencies before, but this was not the time nor the place to beat information out of an aristocrat from a powerful family. "Thank you, my lord," he said, as Francis exited the carriage. "Perhaps your driver could convey us to Longworth's brewery?"

"Certainly," came the reply as the door slammed.

"Relax, Constable," Marcus urged. "Enjoy the ride."

JANE AND GEORGE were about to leave the brewery when their brother's carriage arrived in the yard.

"What the blazes is Francis doing here?" George asked with uncharacteristic vehemence. "Is he coming to see you, Longworth?"

"I have no idea," Jacob replied testily. "I've never met Lord Francis."

Prepared to intervene in an argument between brothers who rarely saw eye to eye, Jane couldn't hide her astonishment when Inspector Halliwell and his constable emerged from the carriage.

George growled. Jacob rolled his eyes. Both men evidently felt as awkward about the encounter as Jane. The policemen could jump to only one conclusion—the three of them had nothing in common and had likely met to discuss the murder.

Halliwell removed his police hat. "Lady Jane," he said with a polite bow.

"Inspector," she replied.

Halliwell bowed again. "Viscount Burnley."

"Inspector," George replied stiffly.

Halliwell settled his hat back on a surprising wealth of chestnut colored hair. "Mr. Longworth."

"Inspector. The Viscount and Lady Jane were just leaving."

"Unless you wish to speak to us," Jane said, earning a glare from her brother.

Jacob's presence always seemed to throw her off balance, and the policemen's unexpected arrival had obviously stolen the last of her wits.

"We'll arrange that for another time," Halliwell replied. "At the moment, we'd like to talk to Mr. Longworth."

"Of course," George said, ushering Jane to his carriage. "We'll leave you to it."

"Oh, just one question, if I may, Viscount Burnley. Are you sure you didn't know the deceased?"

Jane's gaze met her brother's. It was clear the policemen had spoken with Francis. They'd arrived in his carriage. More lies would make a bad situation worse. "Apologies," George muttered. "I did know him in passing, but..."

"I understand," the inspector said with a peculiar wink. "Not the kind of gent a man in your position wants to admit to knowing."

"You're exactly right," George replied, but the stern set of his jaw convinced Jane her brother was lying yet again. The prospect of another interview with the perceptive policeman filled her with dread.

HIS NOSTRILS still tickled by Lady Jane's perfume after her departure, Jacob forced his mind back to the policemen and the possible reasons for their visit. Had they decided he was guilty? Or had they tracked down his vowels?

"Any news of your IOUs?" Halliwell asked.

So, no joy in that department.

"No," he replied. "I don't know where to start."

"Did the Viscount have any suggestions?"

Jacob would have to tread warily. This inspector was no plodding policeman. "No, but he offered to help."

"Why?"

"I keep asking myself the same question," Jacob admitted.

"Could it have anything to do with Lady Jane?" Halliwell asked.

"Lady Jane?"

"It's obvious you two are an item," Walsh declared.

Jacob chuckled. "I wish."

Halliwell put a hand on his shoulder. "Too wide a social gap, eh, lad?"

"A man can dream, Inspector."

"Indeed. So, when did you first meet Lady Jane Yate?"

"You were there. The morning of the murder."

"Do you think her presence was a coincidence?"

A cold shiver marched up Jacob's spine. "Surely you're not suggesting she had anything to do with the murder?"

"I'm beginning to suspect the Yate family was somehow involved with Sharp and his nefarious schemes."

A yawning abyss opened up inside Jacob and swallowed his heart. Lady Jane made no secret of her views on beer and spirits. Could the woman with whom he was becoming infatuated have been involved in Sharp's scheme to destroy him?

Chapter 7

Strategizing

George scoured his brain for the best means to track down the killer. He hoped desperately that a member of his own family wasn't responsible, but his siblings and even his father knew more than they were admitting. What's more, he'd never trusted his Uncle Clarence and his wastrel son, Frederick. Halliwell was reportedly good at his job, but it would be nigh on impossible for a policeman to delve deeply into the Yate family's affairs. His father would quickly put a stop to any police investigation that he deemed injurious to the family's stellar reputation.

If George questioned his siblings, he'd be honor bound to keep any secrets they might divulge. A way to circumvent that obstacle came to him. If he and Jane worked together to uncover the truth, and if he encouraged a relationship between his sister and Longworth, chances were she'd be the one to pass on any important information to the brewer and thence to the police. Unless he missed his guess, Jane would be only too anxious to help Longworth recover the IOUs. The irony struck him. If the plan worked, his temperance-touting sister would be helping a brewery owner keep his brewery. However, he'd have to make sure she didn't become too attached to Longworth. Jane was destined for finer things.

He felt badly about using her, but needs must. After all, the three of them had agreed to work together to solve the murder.

His mind made up, he hurried to the drawing room to explain his plan to her.

"What do you think of the idea?" he asked.

Jane shook her head. "I'm not sure how you expect me to go to the brewery and meet with Jacob. It's highly inappropriate."

Her use of Longworth's given name assured him his plan could work. "Not if you take Florrie along with you."

"I suppose," she agreed quite readily. "Where shall we start?"

"At Sperling's house. Francis is always there. Let's find out if Sharp had some kind of hold over them."

"I've often worried that Francis spends too much time with Jonas Sperling," she said. "You don't suppose...er."

George almost laughed out loud. He knew for certain that Francis and Jonas weren't lovers, but this wasn't the right time to explain how he knew.

JANE HAD NEVER TAKEN a liking to Lord Jonas Sperling. He epitomized the wealthy aristocrat who had nothing better to do than drink and play cards with his pals. He was definitely a bad influence on Francis. Perhaps her brother wouldn't drink so much if he spent less time with Sperling, although that might not prove to be true if Francis had inherited his tendency to over-imbibe from their father.

It was a pity none of her other brothers took after George, who involved himself in all kinds of philanthropic endeavors and charitable works. He'd make a fine earl when the time came.

The Sperling mansion was located in Heaton, not far from Glenairlie, hence the carriage ride was short. The doddery butler recognized George, so they were shown into the drawing room without preamble. They found Francis and his chum playing cards at a high table. Both men couldn't get off their stools fast enough when they entered unannounced.

"Nothing better to do in the middle of the day?" George asked.

"It's not what you think," Francis retorted.

Jane snickered. "You aren't playing cards?"

"My lady, my lord viscount," Sperling said. "Won't you be seated?"

"We will," George replied, taking a seat next to Jane on the settee. "Then you can explain what we're supposed to think."

"We're strategizing," Francis said, earning a glare from his pal.

"Learning how to improve your game?" George asked skeptically.

"For pity's sake," Jane exclaimed. "This is too exasperating. What a waste of time."

"You don't understand," Francis replied.

George narrowed his eyes. "But I'm beginning to."

"Will somebody please explain?" Jane demanded.

"They're practicing cheating," George replied.

Jane was appalled, but Francis and Jonas looked so sheepish, she feared her older brother had exposed the truth.

"Let me guess," George said. "Sharp caught you in the act and threatened to expose you."

Francis whimpered. "If he'd followed through, we'd have been barred from every gaming house in town," he whined. "Father would have cut off my allowance."

Disgust threatened to choke Jane. She hadn't realized Francis was such a fool. "You do realize this gives you both a motive for murder," she said.

"Good grief," Jonas exclaimed. "Surely you don't think..."

"It doesn't matter what I think," George replied. "You'd better hope the police don't uncover the truth. Or better still, you should tell Inspector Halliwell before he finds out. You won't look so guilty if you come clean."

"I agree," Jane echoed. "And if you can assure Halliwell you aren't in possession of Mr. Longworth's IOUs, he'll be more likely to believe you're innocent."

"IOUs?" Francis asked, looking befuddled.

"Who's this Longworth chap?" Sperling added.

Jane and George exchanged a glance that bespoke what both were thinking. Francis wasn't terribly bright, but he was no murderer. Jane decided to inform Jacob of this latest development.

JACOB SUPPOSED it was inevitable that he never looked his best when Lady Jane Yate came to call. A man who owned and operated a brewery couldn't be expected to be immaculately dressed when there was so much hands-on work that needed to be done. He'd never been the sort to stand back and watch others do the work. He attributed the loyalty of his employees to his willingness to work alongside them.

Feeling like a sweaty, ill-dressed oaf, he hurried to greet her as a footman helped her alight from her carriage in the yard. In contrast to his untidy appearance, Lady Jane looked like she'd walked off the pages of a fashion catalogue. His discomfort only increased when her maidservant eyed him as if he were a piece of foul-smelling rubbish.

"Lady Jane," he gushed, wondering why she had come and warning himself to be wary of her motives. "Are you here on Temperance League business?" He could have kicked himself in the arse, were such a thing possible. She was a lady, yet he seemed incapable of acting like the educated gentleman he was.

"No," she replied, with an indulgent smile and fluttering eyelashes that only thickened his arousal. "I've come with news regarding our investigation."

He eyed the maid. "Should we discuss it in private?"

"No need to be concerned about Florrie. She's the soul of discretion."

Jacob remained unconvinced, but he led the way into his office. Admittedly, he wasn't a tidy person, nor did he have time or inclination to organize his office very often. However, Florrie made no attempt to hide her disgust as she cleaned off a chair for her mistress.

"George and I have eliminated Francis and his friend from our list of suspects," Jane declared.

Intent on watching the movement of her perfect lips, Jacob realized he had little idea what she'd said. "Er..."

"Lord Francis and his poor excuse fer a chum," Florrie said. "They're nay the killers."

Taken unawares by the unexpected Scottish brogue, Jacob gaped, no doubt solidifying both women's opinion that he was a dimwit.

"Sharp was blackmailing them because he caught them cheating at cards," Jane explained.

To Jacob, this seemed a frivolous thing to use as leverage, but he'd never had any interest in spending his time playing cards. "However, they didn't kill him?"

"No, and they don't have your IOUs. In fact, Francis had no idea what we were talking about. He and Sperling are like two silly schoolboys, but they're not murderers."

Jacob supposed this was good news, but his brain was busy trying to conjure a way to be rid of the maid. With the Scottish dragon present, how could he ever tell the noblewoman he was drawn to her? On the other hand, what would be the point? She was entirely beyond his grasp and might be scheming to destroy him.

Voices in the yard barely registered, but his body rejoiced when the lady unexpectedly rose from her chair and linked arms with him. The maid glared. Lady Jane's breast pressed against his bicep as she stood on tiptoe to whisper in his ear. He bent his head, foolishly expecting some profession of her regard for him. Instead, she warned, "It's the Inspector."

Marcus wasn't surprised to find Lady Jane at Longworth's brewery. As propriety demanded, she'd brought a maid as her chaperone. What took him completely by surprise was his body's unexpected reaction to the glowering maid. He was ashamed of himself. He'd kept himself chaste since Eliza's death. It hadn't been a hardship. No female had snagged his attention—until now.

"Florrie and I were just leaving," Lady Jane said. "We came to inform Mr. Longworth that Lord Francis and Lord Jonas have been ruled out as the killers."

Marcus should have paid more attention to the reason for her visit, but he was too preoccupied with the maid. "Florrie," he said politely, as he doffed his stovepipe. "I'm Inspector Marcus Halliwell."

"That's Miss Florence MacDuff to ye," she retorted, nose in the air as she pulled her mistress out of Longworth's office.

Marcus watched the ladies go, not knowing quite what to do

with the first arousal he'd experienced in ten years. A Scottish spitfire had reawakened longings he'd buried with Eliza.

Walsh's loud cough jolted him back to reality. Longworth and his constable were staring at him. "Er..." he babbled, trying desperately to regain his equilibrium as he settled the hat back on his head. "Lady Jane mentioned her brother."

"Yes," Longworth replied. "Sharp was blackmailing him and Jonas Sperling. He caught them cheating at cards."

"So, they had motive to kill him."

"What's the big deal?" Walsh asked.

"Being accused of cheating at cards would ruin a nobleman's reputation," Marcus explained.

Walsh rolled his eyes. "Fyking aristocrats," he exclaimed.

"I agree with your constable's sentiments," Longworth said. "But Lady Jane doesn't believe the pair killed Sharp."

"Only time will tell," Marcus replied noncommittally, his brain busy devising a way to arrange another meeting with Lady Jane's maid.

Chapter 8

Albert's Folly

"It's foolhardy, I know," Jane confessed the day after her visit to the brewery. "Perhaps if I explained my views on temperance to Mr. Longworth, he'd be more inclined to..."

"To what?" Florrie retorted, pausing in her efforts to tame Jane's hair. "Close down his brewery? Ye ken that willna happen."

"I suppose not, but he must be as concerned as I am about public drunkenness."

"Maybe, but could there be another reason ye wish to visit the bonnie Mr. Longworth?"

The heat rose in Jane's face. Florrie knew her too well. "Such as?"

"Come now, lassie. 'Tis plain to see ye fancy the lad."

"Is it so obvious?"

"Aye, and 'tis clear he wants ye."

Jane's hopes rose. "Do you think so?"

"'Tis easy to tell when a mon is interested in a woman. The inspector, for example, took a shine to me."

"Halliwell?" Jane exclaimed.

"Dinna fash. 'Tis naught, though the braw laddie does possess a beautiful head o' hair."

Jane had often thought it a pity her kind and generous maid had never married, though it would mean the loss of her position. "I think Inspector Halliwell would make a fine, upstanding husband."

"Nay," Florrie protested. "We're from different worlds, like ye and Longworth."

The youngest of seven children, and the only girl, Jane had long balked at the strictures family members and her rank in society placed on her. "Perhaps it's time to narrow the gap," she declared defiantly. "Fetch my cloak, if you please."

Jacob was glad he was at least wearing his coat when Lady Jane's carriage arrived. He'd spent the morning supervising the refilling of the refurbished mash tun. The odor of boiling malt likely still clung to him. However, there was nothing he could do about that occupational hazard, so he hurried to greet her, his heart beating wildly. The appropriate presence of her maid shouldn't have come as a disappointment. The stern set of the dragon's jaw didn't augur well for a private moment alone with the woman he craved despite doubts about her trustworthiness.

"Lady Jane," he said, determined not to put his foot in his mouth this time. "It's always a delight to see you."

"Likewise," she replied, sending his hopes soaring—or was she simply being polite?

"Do you have more information to share?" he asked, taking the risk of putting his hand on the small of her back to guide her to the office. No corset! Alleluia!

"No," she replied, seemingly not offended by the intimate

gesture, despite the Scottish dragon's glare. "I came to discuss the problem of public drunkenness."

Disappointment flooded him, though the maid's eye-rolling was confusing. What's-her-name, yes, Florrie, evidently didn't think that was the reason for her mistress's visit. "Well," he began, anxious not to sound too anti-temperance. "It is a problem, I agree. However, I don't believe imposing prohibitive measures on everyone is the solution."

"So, you don't think beer and spirits should be banned entirely?"

Jacob worried the question might be a trap, but he had to speak his mind, even if it meant losing the very slim chance of a friendship with the lady. "Prohibition would be unfair to the majority who enjoy beer and spirits without becoming intoxicated. Would you deny the mill worker a chance to share a pint with his chums after a hard day's work?"

"Well...er...no."

He should have stopped there. It was common knowledge many millworkers drank more than a few pints after work. Indeed, his friend, Roger Sandiford, had told him some of his mill's employees never made it home to their families of an evening. Children went hungry when wages were spent on beer and gin. However, Jacob was in full flight and his tongue ran away with him. "History has shown that complete prohibition of alcohol leads to increased crime. Smugglers and bootleggers flourish and there are no taxes to be earned from illegal liquor."

"I see your point," she said.

Astonished that she agreed with his diatribe, he lost control of his mouth. "You have the most beautiful eyes I've ever seen," he said.

Standing by the door, Florrie snarled, obviously ready to flail him alive. He was saved by a tentative knock on the door.

Jenkinson popped his head in and said, "Pardon the interruption, there's a young man here says he's Lord Albert Yate. Found him wandering around outside."

"Albert!" Jane exclaimed, as she rose from her chair. "He's my youngest brother."

Florrie hurried away but returned in minutes, leading a pouting youth by the ear. "Explain yerself," she demanded as she shoved him hard.

Rubbing his ear, Albert Yate's eyes narrowed when he saw his sister. "What are you doing here, Sis?"

Jane's fierce blush assured Jacob she had no good reason for coming to the brewery except to see him.

Elated, he sought to alleviate the tension by extending his hand. "I'm Jacob Longworth, Lord Albert. Can I help you with something?"

"Er...this is your brewery?"

"Yes."

"The one where Richard Sharp was murdered?"

The question took Jacob by surprise, but he tried not to show it. "The very same."

"Why have you come?" Jane demanded. "What does it matter to you where Sharp was killed?"

"I was just curious," Albert replied, his eyes darting to the door where Florrie stood with arms folded.

"Nonsense," his sister exclaimed. "And don't think to escape until you've explained yourself."

As he watched the youth squirm, Jacob suddenly understood. "Sharp was blackmailing you, wasn't he?"

Albert studied his feet. "I just wanted to see where he died."

"To make sure he won't bother you anymore," Jacob supplied. Albert nodded.

"What on earth was Sharp holding over you?" Jane asked.

"I got into a spot of bother."

"You're just a child," Jane exclaimed. "What kind of bother could you possibly get into?"

"I am not a child," Albert retorted. "I'm nineteen. Older than you."

When Jacob was nineteen, he mistakenly thought he could follow in the footsteps of his older brothers. "I suspect this has to do with losses at the gaming tables," he said.

"Francis taught me a few card tricks, but somehow they didn't work for me and I lost money," Albert confessed, fidgeting with the cuff of his frock coat.

Hands on her hips, Jane stood in front of her sibling. "How much money?" she asked, tapping her foot impatiently.

"Five hundred pounds."

"Good grief," Jane cried. "Father will be livid."

Albert rolled his eyes. "Which is exactly why I didn't want him to know."

"Let me guess," Jacob said. "Sharp bought your IOUs."

"Yes, and he threatened to tell Papa if I didn't pay him."

"So, you killed him," Jacob declared in order to see the lad's reaction.

"What? No. I wanted to be rid of him, but..."

"You're a silly boy," Jane said, tousling her brother's hair. "But you're not a killer."

"If it's any consolation," Jacob said. "I'm in the same boat. Sharp was extorting me with IOUs, and I have no idea what's become of them."

For the first time, Albert looked up. "Sharp was very friendly with George. Do you suppose he has our vowels?"

Jacob was intrigued by the interesting question, but something else bothered him. "Furthermore, where did Sharp get the money to buy out all these vowels?"

WHILE MARCUS WAS glad to see the back of his former, now disgraced, superintendent, he wasn't happy with some of his new superior officer's directives. Findley believed that the old-fashioned penny farthing bicycle and quadricycle didn't imbue the public with a sense of the power and prestige of the police. He therefore required patrols and other police business to be conducted on horseback. "Nothing like the sight of a policeman mounted atop a snorting steed to put the fear of God into the criminal element," he crowed.

Having always relied on *Shank's pony* to get where he wanted to go, Marcus had never liked nor trusted horses, and doubted if the sight of him clinging to his mount inspired much fear. Miscreants were more likely to die laughing. He'd heard it said that a horse sensed a rider's fear and reacted accordingly. That was clearly the reason for his disobedient mount's tendency to wander where it wanted. The only consolation was that Walsh was no horseman either.

By the end of the first day, Marcus and his constable lamented sore muscles. Both could barely walk. He hoped that soaking in a tub of hot water before bed and a generous application of embrocation to his nether parts in the morning would prepare him for a second day of agony. Setting out with misgivings about the daunting distance from the town center to Heaton and the Glenairlie mansion, he called a halt as they passed Longworth's brewery. "Two carriages with the Yate family crest," he remarked. "One will be Lady Jane's, but the other?"

Walsh dismounted quickly. "Worth a look," he replied, clearly as anxious as Marcus to get off his horse.

Marcus wasn't surprised to see Lady Jane Yate in Longworth's office. Learning her young brother had fallen prey to

Sharp's extortion was noteworthy, and Walsh did indeed make note of it. The embarrassed youth's hasty departure after his folly was revealed convinced Marcus the boy wasn't capable of murder.

As a long-serving policeman, Marcus had encountered many situations he'd sooner not have experienced. However, the presence of Miss Florence MacDuff threw him completely off balance. She couldn't fail to notice the reek of embrocation. Nevertheless, nothing ventured, nothing gained, so he politely asked her to step into the yard. If she balked at leaving her mistress and Longworth alone, he wouldn't pursue the matter. However, his hopes rose when she thrust her nose in the air and flounced out of the office. Miss MacDuff was a strong woman, worthy of pursuit. The prospect of winning her over gave rise to optimistic feelings he hadn't felt in many a year.

Florence wasn't sure what had come over her. She'd willingly left Lady Jane alone with a young man. She ought to have refused the policeman's request, but for once, her own feelings had overruled duty. She was curious as to why Halliwell wished to speak to her privately. She was old enough and wise enough not to put too much stock in the notion he wanted to ask her out, but he was such a bonnie, kind laddie—and even a spinster could dream, couldn't she?

Trying to control the heat in her face, she asked, "What did ye want to speak to me about?"

"Er...yes," he stammered, clearly hesitant. "I wondered if you'd accompany me to a performance at *The Hippodrome?*"

Her heart longed to accept the unexpected invitation, but a servant's life wasn't her own. "It depends on Lady Jane."

"Will you ask her?" he asked shyly.

She'd never risked her heart before, but the inspector struck her as a man she could trust, despite the fact he reeked of liniment. "Aye, I will."

Chapter 9

Cocoon Of Grief

Jane stared at the closed door of the office, scarcely able to believe Florrie had left her alone with Jacob Longworth—something she had hoped for but didn't think possible. "What do you suppose the Inspector wants with my maid?" she asked, unwilling to look directly at him lest he see the heat in her face.

"I think he's taken a shine to her," he replied, as he came out from behind his desk and took hold of her hand. "But I'm glad of the unexpected chance to speak to you alone."

The promise inherent in his words made her heart race. "You are?" she asked plucking up courage to meet his gaze. The longing in his blue eyes echoed her own cravings.

"Forgive me if I am speaking out of turn, Lady Jane, but I am drawn to you."

"As I am to you," she confessed, staring at the very masculine hand that held hers.

"Dare I hope we might be friends?"

Jane should have left well alone, but, "I'd like to be more than friends, Jacob, though it will be difficult."

"Your parents won't approve of me."

"No, but I do, and that's what matters. We'll find a way."

She spoke from the heart, but her mind recognized the reality of their situation. A relationship between them would be nigh on impossible—unless George was willing to help.

Thoughts of her older brother brought to mind something Albert had said. "I hadn't realized George and Richard Sharp were well known to each other," she said.

She regretted the disappointment on Jacob's face. He was no doubt hoping for a more romantic remark. "I'm sorry. I was simply thinking that George might help us."

"Would you like me to speak to him?" he asked.

"No. I'll approach him."

When the Inspector and Florrie returned, Jacob discretely regained his seat behind the desk.

Jane had never seen her tough-as-nails maid blush before. "Is everything all right?" she asked.

Florrie kept her eyes averted. "Inspector Halliwell has invited me to accompany him to *The Hippodrome Music Hall* tomorrow."

Music halls didn't enjoy a salubrious reputation, but Jane knew her maid well. She never avoided looking another person in the eyes. Florrie wanted to accept the invitation, but wouldn't if her mistress didn't approve. An honorable man like the inspector wouldn't invite a woman to a place of ill repute. The expectant look on his normally stern countenance was touching. "You have my permission," she said, seeing an opportunity for her and Jacob to pursue their own fledgling relationship. "With certain conditions which I'll explain in private."

"FIVE HUNDRED POUNDS!" George exclaimed when Jane told him about Albert's folly the next day.

"Yes, and he has no idea who holds the vowels now," his sister replied.

"Whoever it is must be the killer."

"I was thinking the same thing. Jacob is also worried about his missing IOUs."

George took note of her use of Longworth's given name, but he could hardly object since he'd thrown them together. "You seem to get along with Longworth," he said, hoping she detected the hint of caution in his voice.

"Yes. I really like him, and he likes me."

"What's not to like? You're a beautiful, accomplished young lady who'll one day inherit a substantial fortune."

He regretted the flash of doubt that furrowed her brow, but he had to warn her against a man who might be drawn to her wealth.

"Speaking of money," she said. "Jacob and I were wondering how Sharp could afford to buy up debts. I didn't think he was from a monied family."

"No," George replied, feeling uneasy about the turn the conversation had taken. It was his duty to warn Jane about fortune hunters, but it was his money that had financed Sharp's nefarious schemes. He'd stupidly handed cash over to Richard without a thought of what his lover might use it for. "Who knows where he procured the money."

He hated lying to the one member of his family he felt he could trust, but this didn't seem the right time to unburden himself.

"Another thing," Jane said. "Albert seems to think you and Sharp were close friends."

"Wherever did the foolish boy get that idea?" he retorted, despising his own cowardice.

～

Marcus had no choice but to tell Walsh he was taking Miss Florence MacDuff to the music hall, but he made it clear the purpose was to learn what he could about the Yate family's involvement with Richard Sharp. "It's my gut feeling that the family is somehow connected to the murder." That much was true, of course, but the reasons for asking Miss MacDuff out had nothing to do with police work. He could scarcely believe he'd invited her to *The Hippodrome,* where he and Eliza had enjoyed many an evening's entertainment before her untimely death. But surely he'd grieved long enough? He'd never been even remotely attracted to another woman in ten long years.

He realized how little care he'd taken of himself when his best suit of clothes barely fit—and was ten years out of fashion. Nevertheless, he had no choice but to wear the snug trousers and ill-fitting coat. A man of his height couldn't just go to the tailor's shop and buy off-the-rack clothing. He decided against the waistcoat for fear the buttons might pop open if he breathed out. His police boots were the only decent footwear he owned. He trimmed his beard and mustache, pomaded his sideburns and unruly mop of hair, and hoped a dash of cologne would make up for his less than impressive attire and mask the last lingering traces of embrocation.

He'd received a note from Miss MacDuff instructing him to meet her at Longworth's Brewery, which he deemed a peculiar place for a rendezvous. All became clear when he arrived at the brewery to be greeted by the owner who was dressed in elegant evening attire.

"I hope you don't mind," Longworth said. "Lady Jane suggested we take advantage of your escorting Miss Florrie."

"I don't mind," Marcus replied. "Her father, on the other hand..."

"I know she is beyond my reach, but I couldn't resist the

opportunity to spend time with her. You'll understand when I say I can't stop thinking about Lady Jane Yate."

Marcus was tempted to laugh out loud. He did indeed understand, and it felt good. He'd been a caterpillar for too long. It was time to emerge from the cocoon of grief and soar like a butterfly.

Chapter 10

Escapade

"Ye'll regret this," Florrie scolded as the carriage pulled away from Glenairlie. "I canna credit ye convinced me to go along wi' yer madness."

Joining the Temperance League was the most daring thing Jane had ever done. It risked irritating her father. Arranging a clandestine outing with Jacob Longworth was beyond daring. She feared her heart might beat itself right out of her chest. "I suggest you lose that pout," she replied spitefully. "Lest Inspector Halliwell think he's invited a shrew to the music hall."

Florrie scowled before turning away to the window.

Jane felt bad. Her spinster maid was probably apprehensive enough without the added stress of her mistress's caper. She'd nervously asked Jane to arrange her thick hair into a stylish updo, and Jane had been delighted to oblige. "I'm sorry. You look very fetching. I'm certain Halliwell will be impressed. He seems like an honorable man."

"Probably just wants to pick ma brain about yer family," Florrie retorted petulantly.

Jane hadn't considered that possibility, but it was too late to do anything about it now. She simply had to hope that neither she nor Florrie would have their hearts broken as a result of this escapade. "Cheer up and enjoy the adventure."

She'd deliberately chosen a driver she knew she could trust and instructed him not to bring along a footman. She hoped desperately that Jacob would hurry to help her alight when they arrived at the brewery. She was relieved when he did just that. Clad in an elegant coat of maroon superfine, buff breeches, an embroidered waistcoat, and shiny brown Hessians, he proffered his hand to assist her. Their eyes met. In his blue gaze, she saw the same admiration she felt, and knew she was falling in love with this most unsuitable man. Heartache would be the inevitable result.

RUNNING a successful brewery took time and energy. For three years, Jacob had devoted his life to ensuring Longworth's Select Ales were the preferred choice of discriminating beer drinkers in Bolton and the surrounding area. That hadn't left time for romance, nor had he given much thought to his personal life. He'd enjoyed brief liaisons with various women, but none had set his heart aflame nor aroused his loins like Lady Jane Yate.

She'd dressed simply for this occasion. Indeed, her cotton day gown and woolen cloak made him feel overdressed. She'd had the common sense to realize it was wise not to stand out as the lady she was in the music hall. Yet she carried the disguise off well and was still the most beautiful woman Jacob had ever met.

"Lady Jane," he murmured, as he took her hand and helped her alight.

"Jacob," she replied. "Let's dispense with the title tonight."

He bestowed a courtly kiss on her gloved hand. "Of course. Jane."

His male body reacted predictably when she pecked a kiss on his cheek.

"Let's pretend Florrie and I are just a pair of ordinary girls out for a night on the town," she whispered, cocking her head sideways to indicate the presence of her maid who was preparing to exit the carriage.

Belatedly aware of the nervous policeman behind him, he stepped aside to allow Halliwell to assist the maid.

The situation struck him as comical. Hair done up in a sophisticated style, Florrie was dressed like the elegant lady of the manor, whereas the tall inspector looked like a gangly music hall comedian wearing ill-fitting clothes.

Marcus's instinct was to run as far and as fast as he could. This escapade had been a mistake and a waste of time away from the investigation that he could ill afford. Miss MacDuff politely stifled a snort of derision when she eyed his attire. How had he ever imagined she would want to spend time with a policeman who couldn't dress himself properly in anything other than his uniform?

Nevertheless, he'd faced many unpleasant situations, so he would see this evening through. "Miss MacDuff," he said stiffly as he helped her alight.

"Florence," she replied with an encouraging smile. "And I believe yer given name is Marcus."

The knot in his belly eased a bit as he proffered his arm. "Yes, Florence. Mr. Longworth has invited us to ride in his carriage. Shall we?"

"Aye. We shall," she agreed.

Marcus was the last to board the vehicle. He was surprised to see Longworth had taken the seat beside Lady Jane. There was no choice but to sit next to Florence. He relaxed when she patted the empty seat beside her.

The evening might turn out better than he expected, after all.

A few minutes later, Lady Jane's hand wandered into Longworth's. Both wore gloves but the intimacy was highly inappropriate. Florence must have noticed the heat in their gazes as they stared into each other's eyes. As her mistress's chaperone she'd be expected to object, but she said nothing. He took a chance and reached for Florence's hand, elated when she didn't rebuff him.

She even allowed him to lead her by the hand into the foyer of the music hall. Not that long ago, he'd investigated a gruesome murder that had taken place in this very theater. But he'd attended in his role as policeman. This was different. The air was always just as heavy with the scent of history as when he'd escorted Eliza to performances. The intricate woodwork and timeworn carved statues spoke of bygone elegance. Gas lamps cast a welcoming glow. The foyer buzzed with anticipation.

But long-overdue change was in the works. Maggie Chadwick—now Deschanel—had already begun refurbishing the old theater. Her new husband had been falsely accused of the murder, but they'd put the ordeal behind them. Edouard Deschanel's luxury department store was busier than ever, and *The Hippodrome* was shedding its old reputation as a place for the well-to-do not to be seen.

There was a lesson here for Marcus. It was time to put Eliza's death behind him and make a new life for himself.

Unable to afford the more expensive seats in the main hall, he and Eliza had always sat in the gallery. It gave him great satisfaction on this occasion to produce the sixpence per person so he and Florence could share a table in the main hall with Longworth and Lady Jane.

Chapter 11

Heaven And Hell

Jane had never been to a music hall, but no one who lived in Bolton could fail to have heard of Miss Maggie, the darling of *The Hippodrome*. She was well known even before the fiasco of her husband's murder. Her courage and determination in tracking down the real killer when Edouard Deschanel was falsely accused became the stuff of legend—she was celebrated as a Lancashire lass with true grit who'd saved the Frenchman from the gallows.

Jane was in awe as she watched Miss Maggie charm the audience with her songs and comedy routine. No wonder people flocked to the theater to watch the show. The performers who preceded her on stage were entertaining, but Miss Maggie was clearly the star.

"I'm having the best time," Jane told Jacob. "This is so much more enjoyable than the musicales my parents insist I attend."

"I'm glad you're enjoying yourself," he replied, placing his hand on her thigh beneath the table.

She risked a glance across the table at Florrie who seemed not to have noticed, her attention wholly on the performance.

Jane's gaze met Jacob's as he leaned closer.

"If I've caused offense, tell me to behave myself," he whispered.

Too shy to tell him his touch had ignited a fire within her, she pressed her hand atop his and replied, "You haven't offended me. Just the opposite, in fact."

He meshed his fingers with hers. "I wish I could kiss you."

"I would like that," she confessed, noting that the four of them were the only people in the main hall not indulging in some kind of amorous behavior. Emboldened, when Florrie leaned closer to hear something Halliwell said, she took advantage and pecked a kiss on Jacob's cheek.

Icy heat ran through her veins when he took her hand beneath the table and placed it on his thigh. She had six older brothers. Apart from occasional summer excursions to the beach at Southport when she and her siblings were children, she'd never given much thought to the fact males were formed differently from females. The solid muscle beneath her fingers made her curious about Jacob's body. She recalled the soft hair on his arms. Did hair also grow on his legs? She supposed he had one of those small male appendages her brothers had made no effort to conceal when they were little boys. When Jacob moved her hand to his groin, she realized *small* wasn't the correct word for the warm swelling that made her nipples tingle and sent desire throbbing in a very private place. "Jacob," she breathed.

"My Jane," he echoed.

JACOB HADN'T THOUGHT it possible to be in heaven and hell at the same time. Heaven was spending an evening with Jane, enjoying her laughter, watching her gradually relax in unfamiliar surroundings and play teasing sexual games. He was with the real Jane, not the lady from high society. Hell was being near enough to inhale her perfume, to be mesmerized by the rise and fall of her lovely breasts, and to not have the right to kiss her tempting lips and fondle those enticing globes. His fear she might be his enemy seemed less and less likely.

He worried he'd gone too far in placing her hand on his demanding cock, but her reaction was more than he could have hoped for. Unfortunately, their mutual desire only made things worse. Florrie's frown indicated she was beginning to notice their heated exchanges. He didn't know Halliwell well enough to get a sense of his view of amorous goings-on, but the policeman didn't seem to be getting very far ingratiating himself with the stern-faced maid.

And what of the future? Much as he craved Lady Jane Yate, Jacob couldn't foresee a future with her. It wasn't unheard of for noblemen to wed women from wealthy industrial families, but Jane was the daughter of an arrogant earl in whose world noblewomen couldn't possibly lower themselves to marry commoners. Jacob was comfortably well off but far from wealthy. The earl would likely have him shot if he got wind of their attraction.

The matter of the missing IOUs also hung over Jacob's head like the sword of Damocles. Whoever held them now could quickly bring about his financial ruin.

MARCUS WAS PLEASED when Miss Maggie stopped by their table as she made her regular rounds among the patrons after her performance. She'd begun the practice at a time when she wasn't the last act of the evening and carried it on even though the show was over. "People linger in the hopes I'll favor them with a word or two," she explained as she indicated to the waiter that he fetch an extra chair. "Sometimes, it's exhausting to be popular, but I'm so delighted to see you here, Marcus."

Marcus had to explain to the wide-eyed threesome at his table. "I was best man at Miss Maggie's wedding to Edouard Deschanel."

Maggie smiled. "Speaking of Edouard, he'll be here shortly to take me home in his carriage. He'll be happy to see you."

"Will ye nay introduce us?" Florence said, elbowing Marcus in the ribs.

"Remiss of me," he replied, wishing he was wearing his uniform. Ill-fitting garments turned a man's brain to mush, especially when the trousers were too tight to accommodate his growing attraction to Florence. "Mrs. Maggie Deschanel, may I introduce Miss Florence MacDuff, Mr. Jacob Longworth, and Lady...er his lady, Miss Jane Yate."

"Thank you all for coming. I hope you enjoyed the evening. We do our best to put on a top-notch show," Maggie replied. "Any relation to the famous Yate family?" she asked Jane.

"None," Jane replied, without blinking an eye.

Marcus understood her wish to remain anonymous, but untruths didn't sit well with him. He half expected Florence to speak up, but she respected her mistress's denial. Indeed, her wide eyes pleaded with him not to give Lady Jane away. He feared he might drown in those hazel depths, and had no intention of exposing the truth if it meant pleasing her in some small way.

Relieved when the Frenchman arrived and joined the group, he stood to shake hands with Edouard Deschanel.

JANE IDLY WONDERED if anyone would notice if she crawled under the table when Monsieur Deschanel arrived. She'd often shopped at *Shangri-La,* the luxury department store he owned on Deansgate. Yet, when Miss Maggie made the introductions, he gave no indication that he knew who she was. Either he truly didn't remember her, or he respected her need for anonymity.

She was relieved when he turned his attention to Jacob.

"Longworth? As in the brewery?" he asked.

"The very same," Jacob confirmed. "I'm flattered you're aware of my little enterprise."

"I believe you brew some of the finest ales in Lancashire. We serve them here, and they are very popular."

Pride swelled in Jane's heart when Jacob blushed and modestly accepted the praise. She could well believe he demanded perfection of himself in all his endeavors. Heat suffused her body at the thought this drive for perfection probably extended to his prowess in bed. Goodness! One night at the music hall had turned her into a wanton, but the memory of the hard flesh at his groin refused to leave her. Florrie had once mumbled something about men inserting their male parts into women's bodies, but given Jacob's endowments, she doubted the veracity of this piece of Scottish nonsense.

She didn't pay much attention to the conversation that continued around her, until Deschanel asked, "So, how do you know these worthy people, Marcus?"

JACOB HAD DREADED THIS QUESTION. Deschanel was an influential man in Bolton. It seemed he was unaware of the murder at Jacob's brewery, but the sordid details would all come out now.

"Well," Halliwell replied. "Tonight, I have the honor of escorting Miss MacDuff, who is in domestic service."

"May I ask which local family you serve?" the Frenchman asked.

"Nay," Florence replied. "I dinna wish to offend Miss

Maggie, but I doot they'd approve o' ma presence here this night."

"No offense taken," Miss Maggie replied with a gracious smile. "Edouard should know better than to ask."

Any hope Jacob might escape scrutiny fled when Marcus explained how they had met.

Deschanel gasped. "A murder? That brings back terrible memories, but you have the best policeman on the case. I'd have been hanged were it not for Marcus's dogged determination to find the real killer of my wife's first husband."

"Nonsense," a red-faced Halliwell retorted. "It was Miss Maggie who eventually identified the killer."

Intrigued though he was to learn more of the story that had gripped the imagination of the whole of Lancashire for weeks, Jacob took advantage of a lull in the conversation. "Jane's my cousin, second cousin actually," he lied, though he wasn't sure why he felt the need.

Jane giggled nervously.

Florrie and Halliwell gasped.

Miss Maggie smiled and sent her husband a glance that said it all. They didn't believe a word of it!

"Time we were on our way," Halliwell said, as he rose and held the back of Florrie's chair.

Relieved, Jacob stood quickly and helped Jane rise.

Deschanel bestowed a courtly kiss on Jane's knuckles, giving rise to ridiculous jealousy.

They bade farewell to their hosts, promising to attend the theater again.

A deafening silence lasted throughout the long carriage ride to Glenairlie. At Jane's request, they dropped the ladies off at the rear entrance. Jacob had a feeling Florrie would fire both barrels at her mistress once they were safely inside.

"What the devil were you thinking, lad?" Halliwell asked, as they set off for his flat.

It seemed Jacob was about to be scolded privately.

"I was thinking I'm in love," he replied. "But there's no future in it."

"I know the feeling," Halliwell replied dejectedly.

BREATHLESS AFTER HURRYING from the carriage to the servants' entrance, Florence and her mistress made it as far as the kitchen before the giggles took hold.

"I don't know about you," Lady Jane panted. "I had a marvelous time."

Florence had enjoyed the evening immensely, but felt duty bound to scold Lady Jane's promiscuous behavior. "The inspector was a perfect gentleman," she said, reluctant to admit inwardly that she wished he'd been a bit more amorous.

"I think I'm in love," Lady Jane sighed.

Florence worried she too might be developing feelings for the tall policeman, but it wouldn't do to admit that to her young charge. Love wasn't for middle-aged spinsters. "Aye, well, just remember ye're the daughter of an earl."

"You're no fun," her mistress retorted, as she flounced out of the kitchen.

Florence hesitated before following. It was probably true that she'd forgotten how to enjoy life. A relationship with Marcus Halliwell might be risky, but it was perhaps time she took a risk before it was too late.

Chapter 12

Orgy

R eporting for duty the next morning, Marcus received an unexpected note. Miss Florence MacDuff informed him she would be coming with Lady Jane to Longworth's Brewery at ten o'clock. They would be accompanied by Lords Victor and Edward Yate so that the police would have the opportunity to interview Lady Jane's twin brothers.

The formal note held no hint of affection, but Marcus fervently hoped dear Florence hadn't written him off entirely.

He was grateful for the opportunity to question other members of the Yate family without storming the ramparts of Glenairlie.

Feeling more himself in his uniform, he helped Lady Jane alight from her carriage, not surprised when she bolted for the office. He forgot about her and Jacob Longworth when Florence beamed a big smile as he assisted her. "Marcus," she said softly, a hint of admiration in her hazel eyes.

"Florence," he replied.

Two young men exited the carriage. "What's this..."

"...all about?" they demanded.

"I present Inspector Halliwell," Florence explained before

he had the chance. "Be glad he'll be asking ye questions here and nay in the presence o' yer Pa." She turned from the pouting youths to speak to Marcus. "As ye see, Lord Victor and Lord Edward are twins. They'll be only too glad to assist ye wi' the investigation into Sharp's death." She turned back to the noblemen. "Isn't that right, gentlemen?"

"Yes, Florrie," they obediently chimed together.

Marcus chuckled inwardly. He wasn't the only one intimidated by Miss Florence MacDuff.

As REQUESTED in Jane's brief note received earlier that morning, Jacob remained in his office when he heard the carriage arrive. The reason for her request became evident when she burst into the office and threw herself into his arms. "Kiss me," she commanded, her mouth on his before he had time to react.

Not needing to be asked twice, he gathered her closer and kissed her hungrily, both aware they had but a few minutes to share the intimacy. Her perfume filled his nostrils.

It took only a slight pressure to coax her lips apart.

When he thrust his tongue into her mouth, his spitfire groaned and suckled him. His manhood responded, but all too soon they heard voices approaching. "Jane," he breathed when they broke apart.

"My Jacob," she replied, her eyes full of longing. "What's to become of us?"

When two youths entered, she moved away from him quickly and introduced them as her twin brothers, Lord Victor and Lord Edward.

"I say, Sis," one of them declared. "You look flushed. Hope you're not coming down with something noxious."

"She looks fine to me," Jacob replied, hoping they hadn't noticed the heat in his face and the bulge in his trousers. "Jacob Longworth at your service, my lords."

"Let's get on with this, shall we?" the inspector said as he entered, Florrie on his arm. "Miss MacDuff tells me you two have a confession to make."

~

JANE WAS confident Victor and Edward didn't suspect the reason for her blush. Jacob's kiss had been everything she'd dreamt of—and more. She hadn't known kissing involved tongues dancing together. The memory of their brief intimacy left her wanting more—more kisses, more touching, more Jacob. It was foolhardy. Nothing could come of their relationship, but he was a drug she couldn't give up.

Her brothers may not suspect what she and Jacob had been up to, but the inspector and Florrie obviously did, if the maid's glare and the policeman's snide smile were anything to go by.

"So," Halliwell declared. "Tell me what you know about Richard Sharp."

"Nothing," Victor replied, his nose in the air.

"Never met the man," Edward said, examining his nails.

They cringed when Florrie growled. "Unfold those arms," she demanded. "And tell the truth."

Pouting, Victor mumbled incoherently.

"Speak up, laddie," Florrie hissed.

"Sharp was blackmailing us," Edward declared loudly.

Jane's throat constricted. It seemed Sharp had indeed buried his hooks deep into the Yate family, but... "What did he hold over you?" she asked, mystified as to how these innocent young men could have transgressed.

"We only went there once," Victor said sheepishly.

"At Sharp's invitation, I might add," Edward claimed.

"He said it was a gentleman's club," Victor added.

"Perhaps you can explain," Halliwell said, but Jane had already begun to suspect what they'd been led into.

"You're talking about a brothel," she said hopefully. Their Papa firmly believed every young man should avail himself of the services of a reputable brothel.

"No…er…much worse," Victor replied, shifting his weight from one foot to the other.

"He took you to a den of iniquity," the inspector said.

"Yes," Edward confirmed.

Jane was puzzled. "I don't understand."

"Ye dinna wish to understand," Florrie declared. "'Tisna for the ears o' young ladies."

Jane was tired of being treated like a child. "I want to know what that wretch Sharp got my brothers into."

Wringing his hands, Victor studied his feet, "It was an orgy," he said. "Everyone was naked and doing unspeakable things."

"Like what?"

"I don't think you should ask," Jacob warned.

"Nevertheless, these two idiots will tell me, or I will go to Papa."

"Let's not be too hasty," Halliwell interjected. "Why didn't you simply leave?"

"Well, we intended to," Victor replied.

"But Sharp kept insisting on one more cocktail."

"He got you drunk," Jacob said.

"Well, actually, we think he drugged us, otherwise…"

"Otherwise what?" Jane demanded.

"Well, we wouldn't have taken off our clothes."

Lips trembling, Edward looked ready to burst into tears. "And I fear we may have whipped someone."

Vaguely thinking she had to stop fainting, Jane did just that.

Marcus almost felt sorry for these two naive young noblemen who evidently had more money than sense. While Florence and Mr. Longworth assisted Lady Jane, he took the lads aside. "Where was this place?"

"Dunno," Victor replied. "We were blindfolded on the way there."

"And what makes you think you whipped somebody?"

"We had whips in our hands when we woke up, and Sharp told us we got carried away during..."

"There was a naked woman, you see," Edward explained when his brother faltered. "Tied to a cross."

"So you killed Sharp to shut him up," Marcus declared.

"What?" both youths shouted. "No. We confessed what had happened to Papa. He was going to take care of the matter."

"Aye, 'tis the truth," Florence confirmed. "I o'erheard the earl bellowing at them in his study."

Chapter 13

Revelations

When George was a mere lad, his father often summoned him to his study, where George had it drummed into him that he was the heir to an earldom and should always behave accordingly.

As he'd grown to manhood and ostensibly become the kind of man his father expected him to be, the summons became less frequent and eventually tapered to nothing.

He was therefore apprehensive when he received a note asking him to attend his father in the study. Yesterday, there'd been a lot of angry shouting which George had learned involved Victor and Edward in some way. That might be the reason for the summons, or, heaven forbid, his father had found out about his sexual proclivities. If the Earl of Leyland discovered his heir was unlikely to sire sons of his own, he might...

George squared his shoulders and decided to face whatever life was about to throw at him. Perhaps he deserved to be disowned after squandering his affections on Richard Sharp.

Instead, already reeking of spirits, his father launched into an incredible tale concerning Victor and Edward. The details about his twin brothers' folly came as a complete surprise. He evidently knew as little about his family as they knew about him. However, his father's next slurred statement threw him totally off balance. "I told Victor and Edward I would deal with Sharp. If the police become aware of that, they might think I murdered him."

The knot in George's belly tightened. His father was a powerful man who would destroy anyone he believed threatened the family name—but murder? George had never considered his Papa might have killed his lover. "Surely not," was all he could think to say.

"On top of that, Sharp was blackmailing me, so I'd have more than one motive to get rid of him."

If his Papa knew about the relationship between his heir and Sharp, he'd have motive enough to kill him—kill them both perhaps. Then his father's words penetrated. "Blackmailing you?"

"Yes. He found out I have an illegitimate son."

George's brain refused to digest this new information. Was his father not the paragon of virtue he'd always claimed to be? "Pardon?"

"Don't worry. Philip's older than you, but there's no legal way he could usurp you as my heir."

George realized that wasn't the main reason for the turmoil in his gut. "You were unfaithful to my mother—even before I was born?"

The earl made a dismissive gesture as if shooing away a pesky fly. "I did what many newly married noblemen do. Your mother knew all about the affair. We weren't in love, after all. She understood."

George suddenly had a new perspective on his parents' marriage. He was profoundly saddened to learn he hadn't been conceived in love. "I'm flabbergasted."

"You'll understand once you marry."

George took the only avenue open to him. He laughed uncontrollably and withdrew from his father's study, tears streaming down his face.

~

JANE CAME across George leaning back against the door of their father's study. He looked distraught, almost as if he'd been weeping. "What is it?" she asked, fearing the worst. "What's Papa done now?"

Her brother shook his head wearily. "I can't tell you."

Jane could think of only one reason for George's upset. "He told Victor and Edward he'd solve their problem with Sharp. Did he confess to killing the wretch?"

George snorted. "That's the one thing I forgot to ask him."

"I'm getting thoroughly tired of confusing answers," Jane exclaimed.

"You think you're the only one who's confused?" George retorted angrily.

Jane had never seen her brother so upset. "Tell me. You know you can trust me."

"Right," he said sarcastically. "The little sister who'll run straight to Jacob Longworth and tell all."

"That's not fair," she replied softly, wishing they weren't standing in a public hallway where anyone might overhear their argument. "I'm simply anxious to make sure Jacob isn't blamed for a murder he didn't commit, but the more I learn about Sharp's malicious threats to my siblings, I have to know that members of my family weren't involved in his death."

"You shouldn't care so much for Longworth."

This last cryptic warning was too hurtful. "Follow me to the drawing room, if you please," she demanded, not certain as she flounced off where she found the courage to speak so rudely to the older brother she'd always respected.

Trying to make sense of his jumbled thoughts and emotions, George followed Jane. "I'm sorry," he said, dismayed by the pain on her face. "Papa just told me something that...well..."

"You think he killed Sharp, or had someone do the deed."

"I don't know what to think, but he did have motive to kill Sharp." Weary of keeping his secret and sickened by what he'd learned, he added, "But then, so did I. So did you for that matter."

"As if I could heft a man into a vat of ale," she exclaimed. "I hated Sharp, but...wait...what motive could you possibly have to kill him?"

The moment he'd dreaded had arrived. He stopped pacing, strangely glad to be able to finally unburden himself. "Sharp got his money from me."

"Why would you give him money? Was he extorting you as well?"

"No, he was my lover."

His sister stared, clearly shocked, or perhaps not understanding. Then she narrowed her eyes, and he saw the moment she understood. "Oh, George."

He slumped down on the settee. "I've been a fool."

If he thought she would condemn him, he realized he'd misjudged her when she sat beside him and took his face in her hands. "I often thought it odd you were never interested in pursuing any of the eligible single women who set their cap at you."

"No, I am that most disgusting of fellows, a molly, a homophile, a friend of Dorothy."

"Stop it," she declared. "You're a fine man I'm proud to have as a brother, although...Sharp?"

He buried his head in his hands. "I told you I was a fool. I loved the handsome blighter despite everything. He was just so...charismatic. I lavished money on him. Too naive, I suppose. I finally realized what he was when he tried to proposition you."

"Does Papa know?"

"Good Lord, no."

"Well, he won't find out from me," she assured him.

"I suppose one day I'll have to tell him."

"Not necessarily. Once you're the earl, you can live as you please."

He took hold of her hands. "But I'll never marry. I couldn't deceive a woman that way. My hope is that one of my siblings will sire a son who'll become my heir."

She looked at him coyly. "Perhaps I'll marry Jacob and bear him a son."

"Minx," he replied, though his dearest wish would see Jane's child become his heir. She was the only level-headed sibling he had, and who was he, or for that matter, their father, to thwart her desires if she truly cared for Longworth? "There's something else you should know. Papa informed me he was unfaithful to our mother, and as a result, has an illegitimate son named Philip."

THE BOTTOM HAD FALLEN out of Jane's comfortable world. Strangely, it wasn't George's revelation about his sexuality that had knocked her for six. Perhaps she'd always known deep down that he wasn't interested in women. Being told her married father had sired an illegitimate son sent her emotions spiraling out of control. The Earl of Leyland had suddenly tumbled off his pedestal. She slumped down on the settee and rested her head in her hands.

George sat next to her and stroked her back. "Sorry. I didn't mean to dump this on you all at once. I'm just so..."

"I understand," she replied when he choked up. "It's a lot to take in."

"Papa told me our mother knew and understood because they were never in love. I suppose that's what hurts the most. I've always thought of myself as having been conceived in love."

Jane curled into his arms, taking solace from the brother she loved. "It shouldn't come as such a surprise," she admitted. "Let's face it. Our parents have never behaved like two people in love."

They sat together for a long time, the eldest and youngest of the Yate siblings, trying to help each other absorb their family's stark new realities.

Chapter 14

The Latest Theory

With some trepidation, Marcus entered the cubicle where the Earl of Leyland waited to be interviewed. When summoned to the police station, the nobleman had protested vehemently, but he'd finally agreed to come.

Walsh stood to attention beside the scowling Earl, his face expressionless, but Marcus was well aware of his constable's contempt for the nobility. If Walsh had his way, the Earl, who'd clearly had a few drinks, would be browbeaten like the suspect he was, but Marcus was experienced enough to know that approach would simply alienate him further. An angry peer of the realm could be a vindictive adversary.

"Thank you for coming to the station, my lord," he began, intending to stroke the Earl's inflated sense of himself. "I truly appreciate it."

"Get on with it. Why am I here?"

"As you know, we're conducting an investigation into the murder of a man called Richard Sharp."

"What's that to do with me?"

"Your sons Victor and Edward allege you said you would

deal with Sharp's threat to blackmail them for some imagined transgression."

"Young fools," the Earl hissed. "I did intend to deal with Sharp, but somebody else beat me to it."

"You intended to kill him then, sir?"

"Of course not. There are ways to get rid of an obnoxious person of one's acquaintance without killing them."

"You describe Sharp as an obnoxious acquaintance. You knew him then?"

The Earl scowled, clearly aware he'd walked into a trap. "Yes, all right, I knew him, and obnoxious is the right word to describe him. He had his malicious tentacles in Francis and Jane, as well as in Victor and Edward."

The new insinuation about Jane came as a surprise, especially voiced by her father, but Marcus was intent on pursuing the Earl's involvement. "Was he blackmailing you as well?"

"Yes, dammit, but I didn't kill him."

Marcus realized hell would freeze over before the Earl would divulge what damning information Sharp held. Perhaps Lady Jane knew. "Thank you for your help, sir," he said. "That's all for now."

Nervous about being summoned to the police station, Jane asked George to accompany her. They were both aware their father had also been interviewed, but had no idea what he'd said. Her brother had told her Sharp was blackmailing their father over the issue of his illegitimate son. Learning of this half-brother's existence had come as a shock to Jane. Like George, she felt it cast a dark shadow over their parents' relationship. Evidently, their papa wasn't the saint they'd been brought up to believe. In a way, this new knowledge gave her hope for a future with Jacob, though she'd said nothing of the sort to George.

By the time she, George, Halliwell, and the constable gathered in the airless cubicle, Jane feared she might suffocate, though she wasn't prone to claustrophobia. The constable remained standing behind Jane, and she felt his presence like an avenging angel on her shoulder. She had no reason to feel guilty, yet she did.

"So, Lady Jane," Halliwell began. "Your father intimated Sharp had some sort of hold on you."

Jane gasped. She'd thought her papa ignorant of Sharp's scandalous behavior. "Er...I..."

George intervened. "The scoundrel threatened to blacken her reputation by insinuating he'd compromised her at her request."

Jane was grateful for his intervention, especially in light of what she'd learned about her brother's feelings for Richard Sharp.

"You therefore had motive to kill him," the inspector said. "And you were at the brewery that day."

"I loathed Sharp," she admitted. "But how, pray tell, did I manage to get him into a vat of ale? He was much bigger and stronger than I am. Besides which, my fellow Temperance League members can vouch for the fact I didn't enter the brewery."

"Perhaps you persuaded Mr. Longworth to knock Sharp out with the hammer," Halliwell replied.

"Rubbish," she retorted, her innards in knots. "Jacob Longworth isn't a killer, and in any case, I only met him for the first time that day."

"So you claim," the constable said.

"Now, look here," George exclaimed angrily as he rose abruptly from his seat. "My sister is a member of the Yate family. Her word as a lady is good enough for me, so it will certainly have to be good enough for you."

The constable growled, but the inspector made no move to stop them when Jane stood and sailed out of the cubicle in her brother's wake.

Jacob was again busy, this time with the fermentation tanks, when a worker advised him *two nobs* were waiting in his office. He rolled down his sleeves as he hurried to meet his visitors, and hastily shrugged on his coat when he discovered it was indeed Jane who'd come calling with her brother.

"What news?" he asked, as he shook the viscount's hand and bowed discretely to Jane, who was seated in a chair.

"Halliwell's latest theory is that you killed Sharp at my sister's behest."

Jacob narrowed his eyes at Jane, expecting her to disavow this assertion, alarmed when she avoided meeting his gaze. "Why would Jane want Sharp dead?"

"Look here, my sister used your given name in front of the policemen. You just called her Jane. The pair of you are making it easy for the police to confirm their suspicion you're a couple."

"But again, why...?"

"It's none of your affair," George retorted.

"Actually, it *is* his business," Jane said softly. "He has a right to know Sharp threatened to spread the rumor that he'd compromised me at my request."

Jacob's throat tightened. He now hated Sharp even more than he had before. Heedless of George's presence, he went down on one knee before Jane and took hold of her hand. "I would have killed him for you had I known."

"Good grief," George exclaimed. "What are you saying?"

"I'm saying I love your sister and I intend to make her mine."

"You're mad. However, I won't stand in your way if it's what Jane wants."

"With all my heart," she replied.

Jacob was tempted to take her into his arms and kiss her, but perhaps it was too soon. In any case, she leapt from her chair and embraced her brother.

Chapter 15

Bombshell

George's mother had never been an affectionate person. He'd always attributed her personality to her strict upbringing as the daughter of a duke. The news of his father's infidelity shed a whole new light on the subject. Was resentment the reason for her coldness? If so, he and his siblings could hardly be blamed for their father's sins. He wondered if she knew anything about her husband's illegitimate son. For some reason, he wanted to learn more about this half-brother he'd known nothing about, but he doubted his father would enlighten him. Perhaps he'd sired more than one child on the wrong side of the blanket.

For years, he'd thought he was the only member of this family with secrets. Meanwhile, his parents, Francis, Victor, Edward, and Albert had all been keeping secrets—secrets Richard had made it his business to ferret out. Jane and Eliot seemed to be the only innocents in all this.

Frustrated with his own ignorance as much as with an uncomfortable awareness the Yate family wasn't as upstanding as he thought, George sought out his mother, intending to find out how much she knew about her family's follies. She rarely ventured out of her suite of rooms in the east wing, and George avoided her domain as much as possible. However, needs must, so he took a deep breath and knocked. There was no guarantee he'd get past Ethel, his mother's long-serving maid and appointed gatekeeper. Today was apparently the exception, and he was ushered in without question.

As usual, he pecked a kiss on each of his mother's cheeks after entering her private sitting room. That was as much affection as they'd ever shared. Indeed, he'd never known her to show much affection to any of his siblings, with the possible exception of Eliot—perhaps because he'd always been a sickly child when he was small.

"What a surprise," she said, without looking up from her embroidery. "What do you want?"

She didn't invite him to sit, but he sat in one of the armchairs anyway. "I was wondering if you've been made aware of the circumstances surrounding a murder investigation that's been going on. They affect our family, so..."

"You mean regarding the death of that awful friend of yours," she replied. "Sharp."

"Yes," he mumbled, astonished she knew of his friendship with Richard.

"Your father has kept me apprised of the shenanigans our sons have been up to, if that's what you mean."

"Yes, and that Sharp was blackmailing my brothers."

"And your father."

"You knew?"

"Of course. He came whining to me, just like he did when he carelessly got his mistress pregnant."

Shivering when a cold sweat swamped him, George crossed and recrossed his legs, wishing he'd never embarked on this interview. "You are aware, then, of this Philip chap?"

"Philip Caldwell? Of course. Your father never stops

boasting of his academic achievements while he was at Oxford. He's a don at Manchester University now."

George itched to ask if his Papa ever boasted of his heir's achievements, but his brain was too scrambled to organize his thoughts. He was desperate to leave the sitting room, but his backside seemed to be glued to the chair and he'd suddenly developed a trembling paralysis in his legs.

"But I had my revenge," she whispered conspiratorially. "Your father thinks Eliot is his son, but his real father and I know differently. We're the only ones, now Sharp is dead. And you, of course."

George feared his head might explode as he vaulted out of the chair and hurried away to the sanctuary of his own rooms.

JANE RARELY HAD any reason to visit George's suite of rooms in the west wing of Glenairlie, so the summons to meet him there came as a surprise. She found him slumped in a chair drinking brandy. By the look of the half-empty bottle on the table beside him, it wasn't the first glass. "What's the meaning of this?" she demanded. "What's wrong?"

"Everything," he retorted sulkily. "This damn family, that's what's wrong."

"Well, I agree our brothers, and even our father, have acted unwisely, but..."

"Oh, that's only half of it. Did you know, for example, that Eliot isn't Papa's son?"

Jane had often thought it curious Eliot's brown hair was subtly different from the rest of the redheaded Yate siblings. His temperament was different too, but... "That can't be true."

"Heard it from the horse's mouth, or should I say the mare's mouth."

"You mean…"

"Mama took great glee in telling me. Sharp knew too, apparently, which gives both our parents a motive to kill him."

Jane had never seen George drunk. She understood his pain. He'd often sacrificed his own wishes and desires for the good name of a family that was seemingly rotten at the core. She'd joined the temperance movement in the hope of reforming the drinking habits of her father and Francis, but now realized the problems went much deeper. She too had always striven to behave like the child of a worthy earl, but her feelings for Jacob Longworth ran too hot to contemplate giving him up, especially in light of these new revelations. "I think you and I should start living life on our own terms, George," she said softly.

"Amen to that," he replied. "Join me in a brandy?"

She might need a bit of Dutch courage to accomplish the plan percolating in her mind. "A wee dram, as Florrie would say," she replied with a smile.

It was late evening and darkness was creeping into the yard when Jacob locked the main doors to the brewery. Jenkinson and the other workers had long since gone home. He'd waited all day for Jane to come. Even if the maid or her brother came with her, at least it was something. While working in the office earlier, he thought he'd heard a carriage arrive but it was doubtful Jane would visit the brewery at night.

Having checked the doors were securely locked, he pocketed the key and strode to his waiting carriage. He could always depend on the faithful Henry to wait for him no matter how late he worked. "Good evening, Henry," he chirped.

"Evenin', Master Jacob," Henry replied with a tip of the hat. "Er...the lass assured me tha knew she were comin'."

Puzzled, and reluctant not to get his hopes up, he opened the door. "Jane," he croaked when he saw her huddled in a shadowed corner of his carriage. "What are you doing here?"

He seemed fated to ask the most inane questions. Surely it was obvious what was afoot. Or was it?

"Take me to your lodgings, Jacob," she replied.

He could scarcely believe she'd come to him, but his aroused male body wasn't going to argue. "Straight home, Henry," he commanded, as he climbed aboard.

Chapter 16

Clandestine Tryst

It was fully dark by the time the carriage came to a halt, but as Jacob helped her alight, Jane could see his home was much grander than she'd anticipated. Set in its own grounds, the three-story house wouldn't have been out of place in Heaton.

"Welcome to Deane," he said. "Not as affluent a neighborhood as yours, but..."

When his voice trailed off, she understood. He was nervous too. She'd sensed as much from his silence during the short journey. This clandestine tryst might not have been such a good idea. It was on the tip of her tongue to suggest he return her to Glenairlie, but all doubt fled when he took her into his strong arms and whispered, "I'm elated you came to me." His nearness heated her body. She felt loved and protected.

Uncertainty flooded her again when they were greeted in the classically decorated foyer by a very soberly dressed butler who eyed her curiously as he took her cloak. She hadn't expected servants.

"Don't worry about Banks," Jacob said. "He's served my family all his life and is the soul of discretion. The rest of the staff will be abed by now."

"I suppose he was surprised to see me," she replied, wondering how many servants he employed.

"Yes, you're the first woman I've ever brought home."

She'd compromised him as well as herself. "And I left you with little choice but to bring me here."

His warmth shimmered through her when he took her by the hand. "You belong here, Jane, with me. Come."

She hesitated when he embarked on the stairs. "Don't worry," he said. "I'm in love with you, Jane Yate. We won't do anything you don't want to."

As she followed him, it occurred to her that was the problem. She might want more than she should.

BRAVE WORDS, Jacob thought to himself, worried his desire might get the better of him. It was an ironic predicament for a man who prided himself on his restraint, but he'd never craved a woman like he craved Jane.

Ridiculously uncertain how to proceed once they reached his private rooms, he sat on the chaise and patted the space next to him. She'd taken a huge risk tonight, and he had to make sure she never regretted it. "Sit with me," he said, surprised words emerged from his dry throat. When she obeyed, he put an arm around her shoulders and drew her close. "I confess to wanting you in the way a man wants a woman," he whispered as she cuddled into him. "But it's more than that. I want to cherish you. When we marry, you will come virgin to our marriage bed because every bride wants that for herself."

She looked up at him with those wide green eyes. "Are you proposing marriage?"

"Isn't that the reason you're here? You want to be my wife."

"I do, but is it what you want?"

"More than anything. You're the one I've been waiting for."

SUDDENLY, the obstacles they faced didn't seem so insurmountable to Jane. They truly loved each other. "Kiss me again, but make it last this time."

There was no frantic rush to their kissing. Jacob took his time tasting her lips and Jane followed his lead, pecking, nibbling, licking. As she hoped, he coaxed her lips apart again with his tongue. She stopped breathing and let him breathe for her as she suckled his tongue, then she allowed him to suck her tongue into his mouth. She'd never drunk beer, but supposed his malty taste was from something he'd tested at the brewery. He needed to shave, but his fledgling beard brushed her skin like a feather. He had a healthy, masculine smell about him, though he must have worked hard all day.

The kissing, the mating of tongues, the moaning and growling was all very exciting, so it felt natural to allow Jacob's hand to wander to a breast. "I like that," she whispered, but *like* seemed inadequate when he brushed his thumb over the nipple and desire arrowed into her womb.

She'd always been petite, so she was conscious of the fact her breasts were smaller than those of most young women her age. Now, she ached to arch her back and bare them to Jacob's view, but he'd deem her a wanton.

"Let me see you," he whispered, filling her heart with a sense of rightness. He was the one she had been waiting for.

She watched in fascination as his big, male hands deftly unfastened the buttons at the front of her bodice, aware the silk chemise beneath might as well be transparent.

After easing the bodice off her shoulders, he stared for long minutes before whispering, "Even more beautiful than I imagined."

The most intimate part of her body pulsed with need when he suckled her through the silk. She cradled his head in her hands, purring like a contented cat as she sifted her fingers through his hair. This was what it was for a woman to be desired by a man, one she craved equally.

Before she knew it, he'd eased the straps of the chemise off her shoulders and carried her to the bed.

JACOB SUCKLED Jane's rigid nipples like a starving child. It was euphoric, but also dangerous. Her legs had fallen open as she writhed and moaned. Penetration would be an easy matter...he doubted she'd resist. But he couldn't allow his thoughts to wander there, despite the urging of his hungry cock. But his male pride kept insisting he should be the man to bring her to her first release. Then she would be his and his alone.

With her skirts still in place, he tested the waters by cupping her mons. She astonished him by pressing her own hand to his arousal—his fault for planting the notion in her head at the theater. But the die was cast. She made no move to stop him when his hand wandered up her skirt, past the garter and the top of her hose to the lacy frill of her pantalets.

"Jacob," she breathed. He interpreted her sigh, and the tantalizing aroma of female arousal, as permission to proceed to the opening in the crotchless undergarment.

She nigh on vaulted off the bed when he dipped his finger in the wet warmth and found the pouting pearl of her woman-hood. A few strokes was all it took to send her over the edge into screaming rapture.

Good thing Banks is deaf, he thought, feeling very smug as he gathered her trembling body into his arms.

Drugged on sexual euphoria, Jane was still half asleep when Jacob bundled her into his carriage and gave Henry directions to Glenairlie. "Poor man," she lamented. "Roused in the middle of the night."

"He doesn't mind," Jacob replied, hugging her tightly. "I often work at the brewery until after midnight."

"I'm yours now, you know," she declared, slurring her words like a drunkard. Ironic, given her prominent role in the Temperance League. That thought made her giggle, which brought on a fit of hiccups.

"Yes, you are," he chuckled. "And there will be no other man in your life but me."

"Agreed," she replied, unable to conceive of allowing any other man to touch her intimately. Then, a bit of devilry took hold. "But next time, you must take off your clothes as well. I want to see your body."

"You will, I promise you that."

When they reached Glenairlie, he helped her alight. Holding tightly to the promise, she threw herself into his arms. After a farewell kiss, she hastened on wobbly legs to the servants' entrance.

She made it to her rooms, feeling rapturously free of the constraints she'd lived under all her life—until a stern voice in the darkened chamber demanded, "And where have ye been till this hour, lassie?"

Florence MacDuff had always relished her role as the conscience of the Yate children. After all, their adulterous parents were highly unsuited to the task. She'd never regretted keeping Jane on the straight and narrow—until now. She could hardly censure her mistress for wanting to spend time with a man she loved when she herself itched to see Marcus Halliwell again. She'd never had such intense feelings for a man before, and didn't quite know how to handle the situation. However, she was quite certain she wouldn't have run off to meet a man for a clandestine tryst. Or would she, if Marcus asked her to?

"I've been out," Jane replied hoarsely.

Florence couldn't fault her mistress's rude retort. She was a servant, after all. "I'm sorry I startled ye."

"You frightened me, lurking here in the dark."

"The candle gutted out, but dinna change the subject."

"I went to see Jacob."

"Shame on ye. I hope he was a gentleman. Do ye nay care about yer reputation?"

"Having recently discovered my parents have both committed adultery, I don't feel I have to live up to their standards any longer."

Florence sadly supposed it was only a matter of time before Lady Jane discovered the ugly truth about her parents. "'Tisna *their* standards ye need to worry about. Like it or nay, ye live in a society wi' strict rules."

"Several of my brothers have gotten themselves into scandalous scrapes," Jane replied indignantly. "Father will forgive them and life will go on for them as before. Jacob and I love each other, yet I'll be forbidden to marry a decent, ambitious man."

"'Tis the way o' the world, lass."

"I won't accept that."

Florence mulled over Lady Jane's defiant words while she helped her mistress prepare for bed. She had no children of her own, no life of her own, come to that. Why not contemplate marriage to a policeman she was growing fond of?

The fly in the ointment was this pesky murder. What if Marcus discovered that a member of her beloved Yate family was responsible? She'd known all along the conniving Sharp would cause trouble. Her Scottish mother had told her often enough that men had no control over their sexual urges. She retired to her own chamber, desperately worried her mistress was headed for heartbreak.

Chapter 17

Philip

It was unusual for George to be eating breakfast late. He normally arrived in the breakfast nook before his siblings and was the first to leave. However, he hadn't slept well since learning his parents' secrets, and was still attempting to finish off a plate of fried eggs and bacon when a bleary-eyed Jane shuffled in. "You look like you've been up all night," he remarked, puzzled when she blushed and averted her gaze.

"As do you," she retorted sleepily.

"Can't sleep."

"I slept like a log. Once I got home."

He pushed aside the tasteless breakfast, reluctant to heed the alarm bells going off in his head. "Home from where?"

"I'm going to marry Jacob."

Now George had no choice but to pay attention. "Going to, or have to?"

Anger darkened her green eyes. "No, I don't *have* to. Shame on you for harboring such a low opinion of Jacob, and me for that matter."

There was something different about her—a glow—that

made him suspect she'd been intimate with Longworth. "Weren't you with him last night?"

"Yes, but we didn't do anything to be ashamed of."

George snorted. "And does he know you expect him to marry you?"

"Of course. He's an honorable man and he loves me."

"Not your inheritance."

"Let's face it, George, if Papa doesn't agree to this marriage, there won't be any inheritance."

"So the pair of you will survive on the proceeds of the brewery."

She giggled. "Ironic for a leading light in the Temperance League, don't you think?"

Her humor was infectious. "You're incorrigible."

"But you'll help us, as you promised."

"Of course I will. I admit I'm feeling as rebellious as you. Heaven knows my own love life is in shambles. I think Jacob will make a fine brother-in-law."

"I assume then, you don't believe he's a murderer."

"Correct. I'm beginning to suspect the killer has some connection to our family."

"What about this Philip person?"

"We need to find out more about him."

He left it at that, omitting to mention his intention to first visit the brewery and bring Longworth up to date on developments.

"You're becoming a regular visitor," Jacob told George Yate.

"Apparently not as regular as my sister."

Jane had evidently shared the secret of their tryst, so Jacob steeled himself for a blow, or perhaps a challenge to a duel. George was probably a master swordsman or a crack shot. "You're furious, but be assured I love her."

"I believe you," came the unexpected reply. "I promised my sister I would help the two of you."

"That's very generous of you," Jacob replied, wary of George's motives. Noblemen didn't help commoners who wanted to wed their sisters.

"I'm serious," George replied. "The more I learn about my own family, the less noble they seem."

Jacob was puzzled, but it wasn't likely George would divulge any family secrets. He was wrong.

"Jane and I have recently learned that both our parents have illegitimate children. It's made us think twice about living up to society's rigid expectations of people of our rank."

Jacob's gut twisted. Did Jane see him simply as a means to snub her nose at the rules her rank imposed? Had she thought through the ramifications of a relationship between them?

Preoccupied with his doubts, he barely paid attention to George's next statement. "It seems we have a half-brother who is a don at Manchester University," he said. "I plan to investigate him."

His curiosity piqued by Viscount Burnley's revelation that he had recently become aware of a half-brother he'd known nothing about, Marcus agreed to travel to Manchester with him and Constable Walsh.

He hated the dirty city that held disturbing memories of Edouard Deschanel's farcical trial. However, he was beginning to suspect someone in the Yate family was responsible for Sharp's murder. Most of the Viscount's siblings had been more or less eliminated, so interviewing a new suspect was perhaps worth the train journey to Manchester's Victoria Station.

The Viscount traveled first class, of course, but the Constabulary's coffers would only cover the third-class fare for Marcus and Walsh. Marcus did his best to ignore the unpleasant odors in the third-class carriage. The threadbare seats were filthy, the windows streaked with grime. The broken luggage rack hung at a peculiar angle. It was inevitable his constable spent most of the journey harping on about the injustice of the separate classes and the undeserved privileges of the idle rich. However, Walsh voiced no objection to the comfortable brougham the Viscount had hired to take them from the station to the university.

After a few false starts, they located Professor Philip Caldwell's rooms, where they interrupted a tutorial he was conducting with a handful of students. He frowned imperiously at the interruption. "What's the meaning of this?" he demanded.

"A few moments of your time," Burnley said, with unmistakable authority.

The Viscount's words transformed Caldwell's confidence to stuttering hesitancy as he dismissed his students. Did he know who the Viscount was, or had the arrival of two uniformed policemen knocked him off balance? Either scenario was problematic.

"What's this about?" Caldwell asked nervously, gesturing to the chairs left vacant by his fleeing students.

"Richard Sharp," the Viscount replied, before Marcus had a chance to speak.

"Never heard of the chap," Caldwell said, but his pallor rendered the assertion doubtful.

"We'll remain standing, if you don't mind, sir," Marcus declared. The Viscount's obvious anger was somewhat understandable, but this was a police matter, and Burnley couldn't be allowed to derail the interview.

As soon as George set eyes on his half-brother, two things became apparent. Philip Caldwell was the spitting image of the Earl of Leyland, and could almost be George's twin. And, as was often said, *it takes one to know one*. George had no doubt Philip was a homosexual. He also recognized his lie for what it was. "I think you did know Sharp," he declared.

Any color left in Caldwell's face drained completely. "Now, look here, I don't know who you people are, but..."

"Of course, you know who I am. Lord George Yate, your half-brother."

"Let's keep this interview civil, shall we, gentlemen?" Halliwell interjected, as his constable came to stand between George and the cringing Philip.

George filled his lungs in an effort to master his temper. He prided himself on his control and he'd almost lost it completely. No wonder Halliwell was annoyed. "I apologize. Perhaps we should sit, after all."

Only Walsh subsequently remained standing, notebook and pencil at the ready.

"I'm Inspector Halliwell from the Bolton Borough Police. This is Constable Walsh. We're investigating the murder of Richard Sharp."

Eyes wide, Caldwell gripped the side of his desk. "My Richard's dead?" he croaked, as his eyes rolled up in his head and he collapsed to the floor with a dull thud.

Bile rose in George's throat as the policemen rushed to

Caldwell's aid. It was painfully obvious Philip and Richard had been more than friends. "You treacherous bastard, Richard," he murmured, acknowledging inwardly that he'd been a complete and utter fool.

Chapter 18

Disturbing Developments

"It would be better if you left the room, my lord," Marcus told Burnley, relieved when the viscount agreed to leave.

As he assisted the pale-as-death professor to a chair, Walsh's disdain was writ plain on his scowling face. Perhaps the constable had come to the same conclusion as Marcus—more than a close friendship had existed between Caldwell and Richard Sharp. He'd never understood how men could have amorous feelings for one another, but who was he to judge? He'd been in love with a dead woman for ten years. "So, professor, it's obvious you did know Sharp."

"Yes, we were good friends."

Walsh snorted, earning a glare from Marcus.

"And have you ever met Viscount Burnley before?"

"No, but I know he's my half-brother. My father has kept me apprised. Richard also knew most of the family."

"And you aren't envious that Lord George will inherit an earldom, whereas you..."

"Good heavens, no, although Richard thought it rather unfair since I'm the earl's eldest son."

"Have you ever been to Longworth's Brewery in Bolton?"

"Why do you ask that?"

"Just answer the question," Walsh demanded.

It was unfortunate Marcus needed Walsh to take notes. Sometimes he was too intimidating.

"No, I haven't," Caldwell replied.

"Did you not think it curious that Sharp was acquainted with the Yate family?"

"I admit I was jealous of his closeness to the family that could have been mine."

"Did he seem particularly close to any one member of that family?"

"He talked a lot about George."

"Would it surprise you to learn he was blackmailing several members of the Yate family?"

"Blackmail? Surely not."

"How did he find out you were the earl's son?"

"I told him, not at first of course. But as our friendship became...er...stronger."

Satisfied they'd gleaned as much as they could on this occasion, Marcus advised Caldwell they might want to question him again.

Upon leaving the room, they encountered Viscount Burnley pacing the hallway. "Well?" he asked.

Walsh rushed to reply before Marcus had the chance. "It's possible Sharp knew Caldwell was your half-brother before Caldwell actually told him."

Marcus glared at his constable. When would Walsh learn to keep vital information confidential?

Upon his return from Manchester, George found his

sister reading in Glenairlie's library. "Well?" she asked, as she rushed to hug him. "You look distraught."

"Caldwell resembles Papa," he sighed. "He's definitely our half-brother."

"And? Do you think he killed Sharp?"

"I'm not sure, although he did know him. In fact, I'd say they were more than friends."

"You mean..."

"Yes," he admitted reluctantly.

"But I thought Richard was *your* special friend."

"So did I."

"Oh, George," she said, as she led him to the sofa. "He used you."

"It's a bitter pill to swallow."

"What if Caldwell found out about you and Richard? Jealousy is often a motive for murder."

"True, but the police think Richard may have deliberately set out to ingratiate himself with Caldwell, knowing full well who he was."

"But how did he find out about Caldwell in the first place?"

"I don't know, but we can be sure he was blackmailing Papa over the existence of an illegitimate son. In fact, Papa admitted as much."

"But Mama knew about Caldwell, and it's not as though illegitimate children are a rarity among the nobility. So, why did Papa not want people to find out?"

"Stubborn pride, I should think, and resentment that a nobody like Richard held the power to embarrass him."

"You just gave Papa a reason to commit murder."

"But if I had known about Richard and Caldwell, I might have been tempted to murder them both myself."

"No, you're too fine a person to resort to that. And what about Eliot? Do you think he knows Papa isn't his father?"

"Mama hinted that Richard knew."

"Which means she and Eliot may have had motive to commit murder."

JANE DESPERATELY WANTED to share her concerns with Jacob. Perhaps he could help her sort through the conflicting emotions tangling her brain in knots. However, traveling to his home in his carriage was one thing. Arriving alone in a carriage with the Yate family crest quite another. She had little choice but to take Florrie into her confidence when her maid came to prepare her for bed.

"Are ye mad?" her maid replied to the suggestion they both travel to Deane.

"Please, Florrie. I need to talk to Jacob. He cares about me."

"He's a man. All they care about is sexual congress."

"Is that true of your policeman?"

"Weel...nay...but he's different."

"I can assure you it isn't true of Jacob either. He didn't take advantage of me."

"He didna?"

"No, though I admit I wanted him to."

"Wickedness!"

"It isn't wicked, Florrie. Admit it. You wish Marcus Halliwell would take a few liberties."

"I dinna," she exclaimed.

Jane knew her maid well. "You're fibbing."

A red-faced Florrie slumped into a chair. "Weel..."

"Come with me. We'll be back before midnight, and no one in the house will be any the wiser."

And so it was that, thirty minutes later, Jane and Florrie arrived at Jacob's home in Deane.

"This is where he lives?" Florrie asked, looking up at the impressive house. "Must be richer than we thought. Brewing ale is obviously lucrative."

The elderly butler dithered when they requested an audience with his master. Jane's uncertainty fled when Jacob appeared, ushered her and Florrie into the house, and directed his servant to take the ladies' cloaks. "My apologies," he said. "Banks wasn't expecting you."

Florrie huffed. "'Tisna surprisin' yer butler hesitated to allow entry to two women arrivin' at this time o' night."

Jane was embarrassed, but Jacob took the maid's censure in stride. "I agree," he said. "Scandalous."

Even Florrie smiled at the good-natured teasing.

"I had to see you," Jane explained as Jacob led them into the drawing room. "There have been some disturbing developments."

JACOB LISTENED INTENTLY to Jane's tale about Philip Caldwell, Eliot Yate, and the possibility either her father or her mother was responsible for the murder of Richard Sharp. It occurred to him that his own ancestral cupboard harbored no such skeletons. They may have been common tradesmen, but generations of Longworths had comported themselves honorably. Belonging to the nobility apparently didn't mean the Yates were noble. The amusing thought occurred that their bloodline might benefit if he married Jane. Of course, such a declaration would be inappropriate with Florrie present.

"What's your feeling about all this?" he asked Jane.

"I'm quite sure my father would put a stop to anything that might harm the family, but I cannot believe he would stoop to murder."

"What about your mother?"

"She can be calculating, and I'm not certain if Papa knows about Eliot, or even if Eliot knows he's illegitimate."

"But how would she get Sharp into my mash tun once he'd been bashed over the head with a hammer? That must have taken strength."

"Which rules out Eliot," Florrie remarked with no small degree of sarcasm.

"And we've more or less eliminated the rest of your brothers, which leaves us with Philip Caldwell."

"But dinna forget Jane's cousin and his da," Florrie said.

"Your cousin?" Jacob asked, taking note of Jane's grimace.

"Frederick," she replied. "His father, Uncle Clarence, is my father's twin brother, younger by five minutes. As you'll discover, they're not identical twins."

Chapter 19

The Pitfalls Of Courtship

Pacing the yard in front of Longworth's Brewery, Marcus had no way of knowing if his message had got through to Florence. He'd given instructions for it to be delivered to the servants' quarters, but there was no guarantee the messenger hadn't rapped on the front door of Glenairlie and been summarily sent packing.

His nervousness increased when Jacob Longworth came out of the main building. "You're looking dapper this evening," Longworth told him, an obvious reference to his new suit.

"Thank you. It goes against the grain to accept charity, but Deschanel insisted on having it made for me by the tailors at *Shangri-La*, no doubt dismayed by the ill-fitting outfit I wore the last time I took Miss MacDuff to *The Hippodrome*."

"Perhaps he didn't make the offer out of charity but because he thinks highly of you. You did save his life."

"I suppose, and I have to confess that finding clothing to fit a man my size is a challenge. I just hope Miss MacDuff received my invitation to accompany me to the theater again this evening."

Longworth frowned. "I didn't hear anything of the sort from Lady Jane."

"No offense," Marcus replied. "I thought Miss MacDuff might feel more at ease without her mistress present."

"Of course. You're right."

Marcus didn't have time to worry about the disappointment on Longworth's face when a hackney arrived in the forecourt. He hurried to join Miss MacDuff in the vehicle, his heart gladdened by the sight of her broad smile as he climbed aboard.

His hopes rose when she slid her ungloved hand into his and leaned against him. He meshed his fingers with hers and breathed a sigh of relief.

FLORENCE WAS glad she'd taken Lady Jane's advice to heart. Marcus looked wonderful in his new suit of clothes. It was exhilarating to think he cared enough about her to acquire new garments. His big hand provided warmth and a reassurance of safety. Fear had kept her unwed all these years, yet she'd almost stumbled across an honorable man who would never intentionally hurt her. The promise of a happy future with such a man only served to underline how many years she'd wasted. Yet, the opportunity to watch over the Yate offspring had brought its own satisfactions. She'd learned a thing or two about raising children. That thought made her smile. Perhaps...

"You're beautiful when you smile," Marcus told her.

The dear man would never suspect he'd given her a backhanded compliment, but it couldn't be denied that she'd garnered a reputation as a stern-faced spinster. "You make me want to smile," she confessed, taking the risk to peck a kiss on his cheek. Hopefully, Lady Jane's assertion was correct, and her shy policeman would take the hint.

Throughout the show at the theater, Marcus couldn't get his mind off the fact Florence had kissed him—not on the lips, but perhaps she expected him to reciprocate with a kiss on the lips. This courtship business was fraught with pitfalls, and he was woefully out of practice. Solving a murder was more straightforward, except this brewery murder was turning out to have too many twists and turns. As they made their way out of *The Hippodrome*, it was tempting to ask Florence about the Yate family, but he didn't want her to think that was the reason he'd asked her out. She clearly loved the Yate children, so he could ask her about her experiences raising them. "You've become very fond of the Yate offspring," he said, after they were settled in the hackney.

"Aye, I love children," she replied.

Having long since abandoned the notion of siring children of his own, he wasn't sure what to make of her reply, so he directed the driver to his lodgings. "You can give him directions to Glenairlie after he drops me off," he said.

Her smile fled. Perhaps she expected him to travel to Glenairlie to see her home safely, but that seemed out of character for the independent Florence MacDuff. "Would you prefer we go to Glenairlie first?" he asked.

"Why have ye ne'er married?"

The unexpected question was like a blow to the belly. If he told her about Eliza, she'd deem him a lovesick fool who'd pined for a dead woman for ten long years. Nevertheless, if he wanted a relationship with her, he had to be honest. "I was engaged to be married. Eliza worked in a cotton mill. Cotton dust destroyed her lungs." Strangely, giving voice to his pain eased it a little, so he held nothing back. "It was ten years ago."

Her silence convinced him he'd lost any chance of a happy

future with her, until she said, "I'd love to see yer lodgings, brave laddie, then ye can make me a cup o' tea and tell me all about Eliza."

FLORENCE WASN'T sure where she found the courage to suggest Marcus take her to his lodgings, but learning of his loyalty to his dead fiancée convinced her she'd found a man with a heart of gold. She only hoped to inspire the same kind of lasting love.

When the hackney came to a halt in Turton Street, Marcus took hold of her hand. "Are you sure about this, Florence?" he asked. "My flat is tiny and..."

"I'm sure," she replied.

After paying the driver, he helped her alight. She looked around the deserted cobblestone street, assuming he must live above one of the darkened shops.

"My flat's upstairs," he explained. "Above the iron-monger's."

He unlocked a dingy door at the side of the shop and led the way into pitch blackness. "Sorry," he said. "I'll light the lantern when we get upstairs. Hold tight."

She latched on to the tails of his splendid new frock coat, trusting him as she stumbled up the creaking wooden stairs.

"Stay here a minute," he whispered after unlocking a door.

Seconds later, he returned with a bright lantern. "Come in," he said, taking hold of her hand.

Florence stepped back in time to the small Edinburgh flat where she'd been born and lived with her hard-working parents and eight siblings. She inhaled the same lingering cooking smells, felt the same chill of an unheated dwelling, took note of similar sparse furnishings—a well-worn sofa and a small wooden table, home to a neat pile of books and note-books. A cast-iron fireplace dominated one wall, its mantel adorned with small trinkets and a single candlestick. This was the heart of Marcus's home, providing warmth and a place to cook simple meals, though she suspected he rarely sat at the table to eat.

The floor was made of sturdy wooden planks worn smooth by years of use. The walls were papered with a faded floral pattern. Marcus cleared a space on the table and set the oil lamp there. It cast its warm, golden glow throughout the room.

The kitchen area around the fireplace was tiny. Two shelves held basic crockery and utensils. A single copper kettle hung above the fireplace, a large ceramic jug and basin sat atop a sideboard.

Florence peeked into the tiny bedroom adjacent to the living space. A narrow bed covered with a patchwork quilt took up most of the room. The floor beside the bed was warmed by a rag rug. A small chest was probably for storing clothing and personal items. A galvanized bathtub was propped discretely in one corner. A naughty image stole into her mind. A naked Marcus sat in the small tub with his knees to his chin. Feeling dizzy, she quickly shifted her gaze to the single window that offered a view of black silhouettes of rooftops and chimneys.

The flat was exactly the sort of home she might have expected a confirmed bachelor to inhabit, except it was immaculately tidy, unlike the Edinburgh flat where she'd grown up. She suspected Marcus didn't spend much time here, and of course, he had no children.

Feeling completely at home, she sat on the sofa while he bustled about lighting the fire and making tea after carefully removing and folding his new coat. For a tall, broad-shouldered man, he moved gracefully.

"Just waiting for the kettle to boil," he said nervously, as he tucked a blanket around her legs. "It'll take a minute or two for the fire to get going."

She patted the seat next to her. "Come sit and tell me about Eliza."

By the time Marcus finished his monologue about Eliza, they'd each drunk two cups of tea and eaten an entire packet of rich tea biscuits. The fire had taken the chill off the room, but Florence had spread the blanket over both their legs after slumping against him. Their knees touched beneath the wool. It was agony and ecstasy. He was certain he'd bored her to sleep, but removing his arm from around her shoulders might break the magic spell.

"Are you still awake?" he whispered.

"Aye."

"Shouldn't you be getting home?"

"Lady Jane gave me the night off."

"More tea?"

"Nay," she yawned. "Can I ask ye a personal question?"

"Of course."

"'Tis clear ye loved Eliza."

"I did."

"Did ye ever, ye ken, er... lie together?"

"No," he said, feeling a confused mixture of regret and pride.

"And ye've remained chaste all these years?"

"I have. Foolish, I know."

"'Tis admirable," she countered. "I love ye for it."

His heart raced as his male body responded. She loved him? He decided to take an enormous risk. "I suppose if we're both chaste, we'll need to do something to remedy the situation."

"Aye, we will—after we're wed, o' course."

"Of course," he replied, wondering what strings he could pull to procure a marriage license quickly.

When he was certain she'd fallen asleep, he carried her into his bedroom and tucked her in. He returned to the living room, removed his waistcoat, slipped the braces off his shoulders and took off his new trousers. He draped them over the back of a kitchen chair, turned down the lantern's wick, then made himself comfortable on the sofa. He inhaled the scent of a woman lingering on the blanket, and grinned into the darkness.

Chapter 20

Eavesdropping

When George responded to his father's second request in as many days to meet him in his study, the last person he expected to find there was Philip Caldwell.

"I believe the two of you have met," his frowning father growled.

"We have," George replied curtly. "And I had hoped never to see this bastard again."

"There's no need for that tone," Philip retorted. "Your visit with two policemen upset me."

Determined not to lose his fraying temper, George made no reply, but he wondered why a visit from the police had caused Philip to come running to his father.

"Was it really necessary to involve Philip in this sordid matter?" the earl snarled.

"Well, it turns out my half-brother was well acquainted with Richard Sharp, so, yes, he should be questioned."

His scowl deepening, the Earl turned on Philip. "You knew Sharp?"

"Slightly," Philip admitted, his face reddening. "Just in passing."

"That's a lie," George declared. "I'll wager Richard sought you out simply because you're Papa's by-blow."

"Not true. Richard was a genuine friend to me."

George was on shaky ground. Accusing Philip of unnatural relations with Richard could come back to bite him in the arse. Did Philip know of George's relationship with Richard? If so, he'd have a motive for murder.

His father's shocked response to Philip rescued George from the need to reply. "You consorted with that criminal?" he shouted. "The wretch was blackmailing me, thanks to your folly."

"Perhaps he was also blackmailing my half-brother," Philip yelled, eyes narrowed.

The knot tightened in George's belly. He was about to be exposed, but at least he now knew Philip was aware of his affair with Richard.

"Nonsense," his father exclaimed. "George never puts a foot wrong. In any case, my threat to expose Sharp as a blackmailer would have got rid of him in short order."

The color drained from Philip's face as he blinked. Clearly he'd realized exposing George might end up compromising his own secret. It struck George as amusing. Two *friends of Dorothy* glared at each other in the presence of the father who had no inkling of their proclivities. But how could it be that two sons of the same man had been born with zero interest in sexual relations with women?

The irony only intensified when his father said, "You two will have to learn to get along. I've arranged for Philip to stay here at Glenairlie for a few days."

AFTER THE INTERVIEW with Philip Caldwell in Manchester, Marcus was uneasy. He couldn't put his finger on exactly what it was about the chap that didn't sit well. His association with Sharp was perhaps worth investigating further. He should also confront the Earl with the knowledge that he knew the bastard's existence was the reason Sharp was blackmailing him.

Given his constable's resentment of the nobility, taking Walsh with him to Glenairlie was risky, but he needed someone competent to take notes on what transpired. He almost wished his dear Florence was his assistant. However, her presence might prove to be a distraction from the business of ferreting out the truth. As he and Walsh stood on the front doorstep of Glenairlie, he wondered if he'd be expected to seek the Earl's permission to marry Florence. "Surely not," he muttered. "This is the nineteenth century and a lady's maid isn't a feudal serf."

"Sorry, sir," Walsh said. "I didn't catch that."

"Nothing," he replied when the butler opened the door.

"Inspector Halliwell to see the Earl," Walsh announced, as he marched into the foyer.

Marcus took advantage of the butler's flustered blustering and followed Walsh.

As it happened, Lady Jane emerged from one of the rooms. Marcus wondered if Florence had mentioned last night's tryst and their intention to marry. Lady Jane's knowing smile indicated she had.

"We'd like to speak to your father," Marcus informed her, resisting the urge to return the smile.

"I believe he's in his study," she replied. "Follow me."

Marcus didn't expect a warm welcome from the Earl when Lady Jane breezed into the study with two policemen in tow, but neither did he expect to see Lord George Yate and Philip Caldwell in the study. Angry faces and sternly set jaws suggested they had interrupted an argument.

"Will you ever learn to knock, Jane?" the Earl demanded.

Marcus didn't fault her mumbled apology and hasty retreat. He too felt like Daniel in the lions' den. However, he had a job to do and a killer to catch—a killer who could be in this very room. "I'm glad you're all here," he began, lest Caldwell think to leave. "We have a few more questions."

JANE KNEW it was terribly impolite to listen at doors, but she had to know what was going on in her father's study. Jacob's innocence hadn't yet been fully established. Until the murderer was exposed, the man she craved would be counted among the suspects.

"Get on with it then," her father shouted.

Jane hoped his always strident voice would result in all the participants speaking loudly.

Halliwell cleared his throat. "Although you refused to divulge the reason Sharp was blackmailing you, my lord earl, we believe he knew of your illegitimate son, Mr. Caldwell, here."

Jane's father snorted derisively. "Yes, yes, very good, you've figured it out. However, as I told you before, I had plans to rid this family of Sharp's malicious intentions without committing murder."

Jane pressed her ear to the wood when muffled voices followed this declaration. Fearing there was nothing more to gain from eavesdropping, she hurried to the drawing room, her heart heavy. Clearly, her father had a motive to murder Sharp. More troubling was the presence in her home of a half-brother she'd known nothing about until recently. It was evident her papa had kept in touch with his by-blow, and she'd mistakenly thought drinking too much was his worst fault. If she got the chance, she'd tell this Caldwell she deemed him contemptible for breaking George's heart. She instantly realized the folly of that plan. It was Sharp who'd hurt George, and Caldwell might well be the killer. For that matter, George also had motive if he already knew about Sharp's betrayal.

Solving this tangled web was proving to be too much for her beleaguered brain. She'd discovered things about her family she'd prefer not to have known.

Chapter 21

Shangri-La

"Too dear," Florence exclaimed, when Marcus told her he'd made arrangements with Edouard Deschanel for a bridal gown fitting at *Shangri-La*. She'd been anxious as to the reason for their meeting outside the luxury store.

"Nonsense, my love," he replied. "I've had naught to spend my pay on for ten years. As you know, I haven't spent it on clothes for myself!"

"True, but 'tisna yer responsibility to pay fer my wedding gown. Ye've already put down a deposit on the reception."

"But I want to do this. Can you not let me spoil you? Lady Jane will be disappointed if you don't agree."

"Lady Jane? What have ye done, foolish *mon*?"

"Your mistress is already here at the store. She's more excited than you seem to be."

The crestfallen look on his face bothered Florence. She'd been frugal all her life, a trait inherited from her parents, and possibly one reason she'd quickly felt at home when she'd first come to work for the Yate family in Bolton. Lancashire folk were careful with their coin. However, her penny-pinching atti-tude wasn't sitting well with Marcus. He was a generous man who wanted to spend his money on his bride-to-be. She should count herself lucky, and it would be fun to share a bridal fitting with a young woman she considered more as a younger sister than a mistress. "I'm sorry," she said, taking his hand. "I'm nay used to folk lookin' out fer my happiness."

"Well, get used to it," he replied. "It will be my life's goal to make you happy."

Setting aside her reservations, she linked his arm and allowed him to escort her into *Shangri-La*.

She faltered when lavishly dressed customers turned to stare. "We dinna belong here," she hissed, conscious of her plain attire and Marcus's uniform.

MARCUS WAS RELIEVED when Edouard Deschanel rushed to greet him and Florence. The curious patrons quickly lost interest in them. "Walsh would have something to say about that," he quipped, not surprised his fiancée looked puzzled.

Deschanel escorted them to the Ladies' Wear department where Lady Jane greeted them enthusiastically. The Frenchman suggested the men adjourn to the café and leave the women in the capable hands of the manageress and her seamstresses.

Passing through the glove department, they bumped into Roger Sandiford, the owner of the mill where Marcus had conducted his first murder investigation. Edouard invited Sandiford to join him and Marcus. The three men sat together at a private table and Deschanel ordered coffee and sandwiches. Feeling like the odd one out betwixt two wealthy men, Marcus inquired after Sandiford's wife.

"Thank you for asking. Bea is well," Sandiford replied.

"Expecting our first child any day now. Still working hard to provide relief for our workers hit hard by the cotton famine."

Marcus offered his best wishes for a woman whose selfless philanthropy he admired. He hoped one day to be able to impart news of his firstborn son to the world. Deschanel knew of his impending marriage, but Sandiford didn't. "I'm getting married, you know."

The delighted mill owner shook his hand, asked about his future bride and offered genuine congratulations.

"Any progress with the investigation?" Deschanel asked.

Marcus had to tread carefully. He couldn't divulge much of what he'd learned about the Yate family, but these two intelligent men might have insights he hadn't considered. "I'm afraid it's tricky. I believe a member of a local noble family may be involved."

Since the Yates constituted the only local family that belonged to the nobility, Sandiford and Deschanel must know to whom he referred.

"I can imagine the pitfalls," Sandiford replied. "The nobility isn't as powerful as it once was, but they still control a lot of what goes on in Lancashire."

"It's a puzzle," Marcus admitted, deciding to take a risk. "What's your opinion of the Earl of Leyland?"

"You think he's the killer?" a frowning Sandiford asked.

Marcus made no reply.

Deschanel drummed his fingers on the table. "He strikes me as a ruthless man who'd do anything to protect his family name."

"My thoughts exactly," Marcus replied. "But surely murder would put all he valued at risk? He readily admits to being the victim of Richard Sharp's blackmail, but insists he had other means of getting rid of him."

"Probably true. Why do you suppose the killer chose the brewery?" Sandiford asked. "I feel sorry for Longworth. Decent chap. I know how he must feel. I was horrified when Pickering's body was found in my mill."

"Yes. I haven't ruled Longworth out, but it's doubtful he'd kill someone in his own brewery."

"Unless it happened unexpectedly," Deschanel suggested. "An argument that got out of hand."

"Possibly," Marcus allowed.

"I've heard others remark with relief on Sharp's death," Sandiford said. "Perhaps Yate wasn't his only victim."

"He was trying to extort money from Longworth," Marcus revealed.

"Then maybe there is a whole host of suspects you haven't uncovered yet," Deschanel concluded.

Marcus groaned inwardly. Things had just become more complicated, and he was no closer to learning the identity of the murderer.

"Chin up, old chap," Sandiford said. "I have every confidence you'll solve it."

Marcus wished he shared the optimism.

Jacob rarely patronized Shangri-La—the prices were too steep for his careful Lancashire taste. In fact, he rarely shopped at all. His cook and housekeeper took care of the essentials like food and coal. However, he wanted to purchase something for Jane, a pendant perhaps, a memento that she could wear discretely. *Shangri-La* would have the perfect thing.

He was completing the purchase of a ruby pendant when a hand was clamped on his shoulder. "Longworth," a familiar voice exclaimed.

"Sandiford," he replied as he turned.

"A trinket for a ladylove?" Sandiford asked.

"For my mother," he lied, as Inspector Halliwell and Florrie appeared on the scene, accompanied by Lady Jane and Edouard Deschanel.

"May I see it?" Jane asked.

He'd wanted to surprise her with the bauble, but he could hardly say no.

The clerk opened the box.

Jane stared at the ruby nestled within, then at him. "The stone would suit a redhead," she teased, looking him in the eyes.

Did she realize he'd bought it for her, or was she hoping he had?

"Indeed," the policeman echoed, winking at Jacob.

The wink emboldened Jacob. "Yes, I plan to give it to my mother this evening, when she comes to visit me in Deane," he said.

"Good idea," Jane replied with a nod. "I hope your plan succeeds."

"Come along, my lady," Florrie declared sternly. "We mustna delay these gentlemen any further."

Left alone at the jewelry counter, Jacob completed his purchase, thanked the clerk, and left *Shangri-La,* whistling jauntily as he traversed Deansgate.

JANE KNEW INSTINCTIVELY that Jacob had purchased the ruby for her. That simple truth and the clever invitation to his home later in the evening caused a thrill of anticipation to ripple through her. It was excitingly naughty to share secrets with a man.

Speaking of secrets, Monsieur Deschanel had been obligingly discrete. He'd mentioned nothing about meeting her at *The Hippodrome* with Jacob. It was no wonder his store was so successful. The well-to-do placed a high value on discretion.

Chapter 22

A Clever Plan

"I think it's a clever plan," Jane told Florrie, as her maid helped her don a pelisse.

"I ne'er kent ye ha'e such a devious mind."

"It's not devious. In fact, it's straightforward. You and I will leave in the carriage. We'll pick up Inspector Halliwell at his flat. You'll drop me off at Jacob's house in Deane and carry on to *The Hippodrome*. You're an affianced couple, so there's naught wrong with that."

"I dinna like to point out the wee flaw in yer plan, but ye and Mr. Longworth are nay engaged to be married."

"But we soon will be—married that is."

Florrie rolled her eyes.

"I don't appreciate your attitude, Miss MacDuff," Jane huffed. "I'm providing you an opportunity to spend an evening with the man you love."

Florrie sighed. "Aye, I suppose ye're right."

"You do love the inspector, don't you?"

"He's a grand lad."

"But do you love him?"

"I ne'er thought to utter these words, but this old spinster is head o'er heels!"

"Isn't it wonderful to be in love?" Jane exclaimed.

Arm in arm, and still laughing, they made their way to the servants' quarters, and thence to the stables where their trusty driver awaited them.

Jacob insisted Banks retire early, just in case Jane did manage to escape Glenairlie. Gift-wrapped jewelry box in hand, he paced the tiled foyer, his hopes fading as the minutes ticked by.

Finally hearing the crunch of carriage wheels on the gravel, he thrust open the door in time to see Inspector Halliwell assist Jane to alight.

"This isn't exactly proper," the policeman said when they reached the door. "You're both involved in a murder investigation that I'm conducting and I'm assisting you with an improper assignation."

"Thank you, Inspector," Jane replied. "We won't tell if you don't."

Seemingly not certain how to respond to this teasing remark, Halliwell doffed his shiny new top hat and returned to the carriage.

"You're naughty," Jacob accused as he swept Jane into his arms and kicked the door closed.

"Not as naughty as my maid," Jane replied playfully. "Imagine, not yet married and she's going off to the theater with her lover."

"I doubt Halliwell will do anything improper."

"Probably not, though I suspect Florrie would like him to."

"What makes you say that?" he asked as he escorted her upstairs.

"She's a woman in love. Women in love crave a lover's touch."

Intrigued by her declaration, he paused on the landing and took her back into his arms. "Do you crave my touch?"

"All the time," she confessed. "But you've seen parts of me I've never allowed anyone to see. Tonight, I want to see all of *you*."

Jacob's heart and body rejoiced. "Your wish is my command, my lady."

"Good. When we're both naked, then you can give me my ruby."

Jacob chuckled. His initial impression of Lady Jane Yate had been spot-on. Spitfire indeed.

"Let's not waste time," Jane told Jacob. "I'll undress while you do the same."

"No," Jacob replied. "Taking off your clothes is arousing for me."

Jane wasn't used to being contradicted, but Jacob might be right. Undressing a man would be nerve-wracking but thrilling at the same time. "Very well," she agreed.

"I'll start," he said, unfastening the buttons of her bodice. "Front fasteners are very convenient."

"Florrie said as much."

He laughed. "Your very proper maid, you mean."

Jane realized she'd revealed things about her maid she shouldn't have, but she swallowed her regret when Jacob slipped the bodice from her shoulders and stared.

"I love this silk chemise," he quipped. "Very revealing. But you're wearing a corset this evening."

"Yes. Florrie suggested a corset pushes up…"

She lost track of what she was about to say when he brushed his thumbs over both pouting nipples, and her most intimate female part pulsed with need.

"I'm beginning to see a whole new side of Florence MacDuff," he whispered.

"What?" she replied, lost in sensation.

"My turn," he said, shrugging off his coat and kicking off his slippers. "Waistcoat and shirt first."

Nostrils flared, Jane fiddled with the buttons of the waistcoat like a drunkard, then slid the garment off his body. Impatient to see his naked chest, she was grateful when he pulled the shirt over his head.

He inhaled sharply when she pressed her thumbs to the flat brown nipples.

"There's hair on your chest," she said softly, sifting her fingers through the golden whorls.

"But, you've six brothers," he replied with a chuckle.

"Yes, but I haven't seen them undressed since we went to the beach at Southport when they were little boys."

"Let's get this corset undone," he said.

Reluctant to tear her gaze away from the taut ridges of his chest, she turned her back to him so he could undo the laces.

"That feels better," she sighed, as he slipped the laces free and tossed the corset aside.

He turned her to face him and started on the fastenings of her skirt, all the while gazing at her scantily covered breasts. The skirt slid off her hips and pooled at her feet, leaving her clad in nothing but the chemise, her pantalets, and knee boots.

Tempted to remove the chemise herself, she hesitated when he said, "Trousers next."

Jacob strove to sound flippant about the undressing, but his brain couldn't keep up with the saucy images of Jane clad in nothing but pantalets and knee boots, or knee boots and nothing else, or...

Jaw clenched, he reminded himself he had to warn Jane about his size. God had been generous with his physical endowments. He loved that she was playing the part of a wanton when it came to sexual matters, but he wasn't fooled. She was an innocent trying her best to appear sophisticated, but the sight of his fully aroused cock might...

Too late, he realized, when Jane shoved his trousers over his hips and gawked at the arousal tenting his smalls. "Let me explain," he began.

Any explanatory words refused to emerge from his dry throat when Jane curled both hands around him and said, "I want to touch you like you touched me."

It was like lighting the blue paper on a firework. At least that's the way he later rationalized how, within thirty seconds, they were both stark naked and lying on the bed. He didn't need Jane to keep on her pantalets nor her boots. Her lithe body was sufficient to harden him to the point of pain. The torture continued when she put her mouth on him and suckled.

Teetering on the edge of losing complete control, he sifted his fingers through her burnished glory and resolved to do everything in his power to make this incredible woman his.

Jane heard a distant clock chime somewhere in Jacob's house. Two o'clock. Listening to her beloved snoring softly beside her, she absently twirled her fingertips in the sticky liquid between her naked breasts. She would never forget Jacob's cry of ecstasy when his essence exploded from his magnificent male part, nor his hoarse promise it would be even better when he could thrust inside her.

It was difficult to imagine how anything could be better than the rapture wrought by Jacob's clever tongue on her breasts. Also important was the chance to ask his advice about the involvement of her family in Sharp's schemes. He listened intently, but only offered the opinion they should sleep on the matter. She was confident he'd keep the secrets she told him.

She squinted at the ruby he'd fastened around her neck. It wasn't the most expensive piece of jewelry she owned, but it meant more to her than all the Yate diamonds, emeralds and sapphires she was destined to inherit.

Despite her euphoria, sleep proved elusive. Jacob had insisted he intended to ask her father for her hand in marriage. She feared that would sound the death knell for their relationship.

Chapter 23

Loose Ends

After his discussion with Sandiford and Deschanel, Marcus pondered the distinct possibility Longworth had shoved Sharp into the mash tun in the course of a heated argument. He'd taken a liking to the young brewery owner and couldn't really believe he might be a killer, but it was his duty to investigate every angle. After all, Longworth did have a strong motive. He should have known better than to mention this to his superior, who immediately ordered Longworth's arrest. He'd hoped his new superintendent would prove to be a more sensible man than his predecessor, but it seemed Findley was also prone to jumping to conclusions.

Feeling decidedly ambivalent about arresting the brewer, Marcus dismounted when he and Walsh came across Longworth in the brewery's cobblestone yard. He and several of his workers were loading barrels onto a beer wagon. A magnificent dray horse stood in the traces. A man Marcus assumed to be the driver held the bridle while the impressive animal munched an apple.

The police horses grew skittish, so Marcus asked Walsh to

141

take them away from the dray horse. "Wait in the street," he instructed, earning the constable's scowl.

"I don't care much for horses," Marcus told the driver. "But that's a grand specimen you've got there."

"Aye," the driver replied, politely removing his cap. "Daisy's a champion."

"Can I help you, Inspector?" Longworth called from where he stood with legs braced atop the wagon. "We're rather busy, as you see."

"A moment of your time," Marcus replied.

Longworth jumped down from the wagon. "This shipment's for *The Nag's Head* on Deansgate."

"I know it well," Marcus replied, recalling a time he could have jumped down from the wagon with the same athletic grace. Those days were long gone.

"Then you know how testy the landlord can be."

"I do, but I wanted to ask about your vowels. How much money do you owe?"

Longworth narrowed his eyes. "The IOUs amount to a substantial sum, but why do you ask?"

"And no one has pressed you for payment?"

"No, but I can assure you I didn't murder Sharp. I may have wanted to strangle him but..."

"So, you didn't argue with him up on the platform near the mash tun?"

"Jenkinson and the others can attest that I did indeed have a heated discussion with him in my office, but we never went near the mash tun."

"You've no objection then if we question your workers?"

"None. However..."

Arresting Longworth would be a waste of police time, but the young brewer knew something.

JACOB DITHERED. Jane had told him her family's secrets in confidence, but it was disturbingly obvious the police still considered him a suspect. Surely she wouldn't fault him for wanting to deflect suspicion away from himself? "Have you eliminated all the members of the Yate family?" he asked.

"Sounds like you know something we don't," Walsh replied.

"You're already aware of Philip Caldwell."

The Inspector nodded. "Yes, he's the Earl's by-blow."

"But did you know about Eliot Yate?"

"What about him?"

"He's not the Earl's son."

Walsh mumbled something derogatory about loose morals and entitlement, earning a glare from Halliwell.

"Who told you this?" the Inspector asked. "Never mind. I can probably guess. Is he aware he's not the Earl's son?"

"That I don't know, but Miss MacDuff might."

The inspector's frown and the stern set of his jaw were a clear indication he would prefer not to ask Lady Jane's maid. Or perhaps Walsh didn't know of his relationship with her, and Halliwell wanted to keep it that way.

"Or you could ask the Countess," he suggested, suspecting the policeman would rather not question a noblewoman known for her blistering temper and disdain for commoners.

That thought brought home to him the uphill battle he faced in seeking to marry Jane.

MARCUS KNEW IT WAS COWARDLY, but he decided to enlist the help of Lady Jane to arrange an interview with the Countess of

Leyland. He deemed it more likely he and Walsh wouldn't be turned away from Glenairlie if they asked to speak to Lady Jane.

The plan worked smoothly until they were in the drawing room with the youngest member of the family.

"You wish to speak to my mother?" she asked incredulously. "And you want me to arrange it?"

"It's important we speak to the Countess."

"About what?"

Marcus had assumed Longworth had learned of Eliot Yate's dubious parentage from Lady Jane, but perhaps she didn't know. Although, who else could have told Longworth? Marcus decided to err on the side of caution. "A few loose ends need to be tidied up."

"My mother won't appreciate being thought of as a loose end," Lady Jane said.

It dawned on him then that she was afraid of her mother's temper and it saddened him. With two adulterous parents who prized their noble name but behaved ignobly, it was a wonder she'd turned out to be the pleasant young woman that she was, if somewhat willful. Her relationship with Longworth would eventually come to nothing, but he had to admire her for not conforming to the normal dictates of her class. "I will take full responsibility for my actions," he replied.

Lady Jane considered what he'd said for a few moments, then said, "Very well, I'll take you to her sitting room."

HAVING SUCCESSFULLY NAVIGATED her way past Ethel, Jane fulfilled her obligation, retreating from her mother's sitting room quickly once anger flared in the Countess's face. Her mother had never treated her with the same loving indulgence lavished on her by her father. Given what she'd learned about her parents, Jane perhaps had a better understanding of her mother's cold demeanor, but her children weren't to blame for another generation's infidelity. She resolved to be a loving mother to any children she and Jacob might sire.

It was obvious the policemen had come to ask questions about Eliot, and they could only have learned of his illegitimacy from Jacob. So much for promises of confidentiality. "Thank goodness I didn't tell him about George's proclivities," she murmured, pressing her ear to the door.

"This eavesdropping must stop," she muttered. It was rude, as well as unladylike, but she had to know what was going on.

"I refuse to be questioned like some common criminal," her mother shouted. "Get out."

To his credit, Halliwell stood his ground. "I am conducting a murder inquiry, my lady, and I'm obliged to follow every lead. You can understand that."

"Very well, get on with it," the Countess replied. "I suppose you've come to ask about Eliot. That's the last time I confide in George."

Pressing her ear more closely to the door, Jane gasped. Was her mother about to reveal the identity of Eliot's father?

Chapter 24

Unladylike Pursuits

Florence was torn. She owed the Yate family a great deal. The Earl and Countess had seen to her welfare from the very beginning of her employment at the age of eighteen. She was fortunate to have a spacious bedroom and had always been treated with respect. It was a far cry from the overcrowded flat in Edinburgh. Fellow household staff members had related horror stories about previous experiences in other grand houses. She'd eventually been promoted from maid-of-all-work to lady's maid to the Countess and subsequently to Lady Jane. She'd played a role in raising all the Yate children, and liked to think she'd had more positive influence on them than their careless parents. George was an awkward thirteen-year-old when she'd arrived, and she'd watched him grow into a handsome, upright man. It rankled that the Earl lavished more attention on his illegitimate son than on his bright, capable heir. The Countess pampered Eliot. The truth of his parentage had never been spoken of, but lady's maids tended to know things, and Florence had kept the Countess's secret. Her loyalty lay with the family, but she had a new duty—to assist Marcus in solving the murder. Success would be a feather in his cap. Failure might result in demotion. She was privy to information about the family that might help with the investigation.

She and Marcus had fallen into the habit of patronizing *The Hippodrome* once a week on Saturday evening—since Sunday was her day off. It felt grand to sit in the main hall and not in the gallery. She loved the thrill of spending the nights at his flat after the performances. They kissed and cuddled on the sofa. Sensing he was nervous about offending her, she'd eventually taken his hand and placed it on her breast. They left the intimacy at that for the moment, though she had to admit his touch kindled a desire for more. She often bit back the temptation to offer to scrub his back if he'd a mind to take a bath in the wee tub.

He carried her into the bedroom when she fell asleep, then retired to sleep on the sofa. She loved waking in bed linens that smelled of him and making his breakfast. It was a glimpse into an uncomplicated but happy future.

"I ken ye're reluctant to ask me, so I want to tell ye something about the Yates ye might not ken," she told him one evening.

"I doubt you can tell me anything we haven't already discovered," he sighed in reply.

"Have ye questioned Frederick and his father, Clarence Yate?"

"No, but the Countess revealed Clarence is Eliot's father."

"Ye did weel to prise that information from her."

"I didn't have to browbeat her to tell me. She gave up the truth quite readily and confessed that Sharp knew. However, I still don't know if Eliot and the Earl are aware of his parentage."

"I'd say the Earl suspects. Eliot is so obviously different in appearance and temperament from the rest of his siblings. 'Twouldna surprise me if the Countess told him out of spite."

"I'm starting to understand Walsh's disdain for the nobility. I have less and less regard for this family."

"Aye, but ye canna blame the children for their parents' failings."

"In any case, I don't see the Countess as a murderess, unless she coerced someone else to kill Sharp."

"Nay, the Earl and Countess might not be the ideal married couple, but she would support any plan her husband came up with to get rid o' Sharp."

"In other words, they would connive together to bring about his ruin."

"Exactly. Making him a social outcast would give them more satisfaction than killin' him."

"Probably true, and I haven't discovered a motive for Clarence Yate or his son to kill Sharp. Did they even know the wretch?"

"Lady Jane would ken," she replied.

"I THOUGHT I might find you here at the brewery," the inspector told Jane as Jacob lifted her down from the beer wagon. She'd have kissed him if the policeman hadn't come upon them.

Surprised and somewhat embarrassed to be caught engaging in unladylike pursuits, Jane nevertheless took the barb in good humor. "Jacob is teaching me the finer points of brewing and delivering excellent beer."

"That's what I assumed," he replied with a wink.

"How can I help you?" she asked, dusting off her skirts.

"Talk to me about your cousin Frederick and his father."

"I'd rather not," she replied, wrinkling her nose. "I avoid them whenever possible."

"Why is that?"

Jane had to be cautious. Her cousin and uncle were part of the Yate clan, after all, and Jacob was listening. "Frederick is afflicted with a wandering-hands problem."

Halliwell nodded. "I'm afraid it's an affliction from which many young men suffer."

She hesitated before continuing. "He wants me to marry him and can't accept that I find the notion unpalatable."

Beside her, fists clenched, Jacob tensed.

Halliwell wouldn't let the matter drop. "So, he's upset with you."

Jane reached for Jacob's hand, knowing what she was about to reveal would rile him further. "I don't know if *upset* is the right word. He thinks to force me into marriage."

Jacob meshed his fingers with hers so tightly it was almost painful.

"Malevolent, then," Halliwell said.

Jane decided she might as well tell the truth. "A trait he inherited from his father."

"I understand Clarence is your father's twin brother."

Jane hesitated. Having overheard the interview between Halliwell and her mother, she had learned to her disgust that the Countess of Leyland had committed adultery with her uncle. But the inspector didn't know she'd eavesdropped on the conversation, and neither did Jacob. "I've never liked nor trusted my uncle," she said, hoping that would be enough to convey her true feelings to both men.

"One last question," Halliwell said. "Were your uncle and cousin acquainted with Richard Sharp?"

Jane thought back. "They'll deny it, but I think they knew him."

❧

SSATISFIED HE'D GLEANED as much as Lady Jane was willing to tell him about her relatives, Marcus rejoined Walsh waiting in the street with the horses. The young constable sulked when given a task he obviously resented, but Marcus had been reluctant to bring the police horses into the forecourt given their previous reaction to the dray horse. Longworth's employee had assured him Daisy was a champion, but Marcus wouldn't trust his own horse as far as he could throw him! Or her?

The amusing realization he hadn't bothered to check brought a smile to his face.

"Progress?" Walsh asked, apparently misconstruing the reason for his good humor.

"I think we'll interview Clarence Yate next," Marcus replied.

"Who's he?"

"An uncle of the siblings we've already eliminated."

"Probably another wild goose chase," Walsh muttered.

They mounted their steeds and set off to locate Clarence Yate.

Chapter 25

Incriminating Evidence

In the course of Marcus making enquiries about contacting Clarence Yate, the man himself appeared at the police station and asked to speak to him. Walsh ushered him into the cubicle that served as an interview room.

"You wish to make a statement?" Marcus asked.

"Er...yes."

"You seem uncertain."

Yate leaned forward as if about to inform on some secret conspiracy. "You wouldn't understand, but family loyalty is paramount among people of our class."

Marcus expected Walsh to react to this patronizing remark, but his constable's facial expression betrayed nothing. "If you have something to tell me about a member of your family, you must remember this is a murder enquiry. I suggest you get it off your chest."

"It's about my brother, you see."

"The earl?"

"We're twins—fraternal, of course—so I sensed from the outset he was hiding something."

Marcus refrained from mentioning the big lie Clarence Yate had kept hidden for years. "And what is he hiding?"

"He has Albert's IOUs in his possession."

"And how do you know this?"

"The Countess told me."

Given what he'd learned about Eliot Yate's parentage, Marcus could readily believe this assertion. "What about Jacob Longworth's vowels. Does he have those?"

"I have no idea. The Countess was anxious for me to stop worrying about my nephew's debts."

A thousand questions buzzed in Marcus's brain, but it was unlikely Yate would answer most of them truthfully. His responsibility now was to find out if the allegation was true.

"What's your opinion?" he asked Walsh after the nobleman had left.

"Slippery character," his constable replied. "And a snob, but that goes without saying."

"Yes, but if what he says is true..."

"Then the Earl is probably the killer."

"He'd be hanged if found guilty. And Burnley would become the earl."

Walsh tapped his chin. "Or Clarence Yate might have a stronger claim."

"A tangled web, indeed."

TRUE TO HIS WORD, George welcomed Longworth to Glenairlie and agreed to escort him and Jane to seek his father's approval to marry Jane. As he, Jane, and Longworth approached the Earl's study, he heard a commotion. Always strident, his father's voice could probably be heard in the next county. "This might not be the best time to ask for Jane's hand," he told Jacob.

"Who's in there with him?" Longworth asked.

"Sounds like Halliwell and his constable."

"Oh, dear," Jane murmured, disappointment marring her lovely features.

"I'll go in and see if I can't calm the waters," George suggested. "Wait in the drawing room."

He tapped lightly and entered without waiting for permission.

His red-faced father glared at him. "I suppose you engineered this travesty," he charged. "Can't wait to get me out of the way."

"If you'll allow me..." Halliwell began.

"To search my desk? Absolutely not," the Earl retorted.

"I'm not sure what this is about, Papa, but..."

"Don't Papa me. You made up this preposterous story."

"It was your twin brother told us," the constable shouted.

George's father gaped, obviously stunned into silence, but then he rallied. "That fool has always been jealous of me. Wasn't enough he cuckolded me. I'll show you, just to prove him wrong."

He yanked open a drawer and stared.

Halliwell reached into the drawer and pulled out a small signed and sealed document. "The proof that your son Albert owed Sharp money, I believe, my lord."

ALARMED by the brouhaha going on in the foyer, Jane hurried to ease open the door of the drawing room. "The police are taking Father away," she told Jacob, who'd come to stand behind her.

"Surely they can't think the Earl is the murderer," he replied, opening the door wider.

"I'm afraid they found evidence to suggest he killed Sharp," George said as he joined them.

"What evidence?" Jane asked, clinging to Jacob for support lest she swoon yet again. This nasty murder business was turning her into a simpering nitwit.

"Albert's vowels," George explained. "A note demanding our little brother pay Sharp six hundred pounds."

"What about *my* IOUs?" Jacob asked. "Did they find those as well?"

"No. Strange, don't you think?"

"What's going on?" Jane's mother asked, as she flounced into the drawing room.

"Good grief," Jane whispered to Jacob. "It's the first time in months I've seen her outside her suite of rooms."

"Papa has been taken in for questioning," George explained, after telling her about the incriminating note. "The police came expressly to search Papa's desk."

"It sounds to me like someone knew the evidence was there," the Countess replied.

"You're right, my lady," Jacob said. "It seems very convenient."

"And who are you?" the Countess asked, looking at Jacob as if he were something the cat dragged in.

Jane decided to take the bull by the horns. "Mama, I'd like you to meet my fiancé, Jacob Longworth."

"Rubbish," came the rude reply. "You cannot marry **him**. We'll discuss this nonsense another time. The immediate need is to track down how that note got into my husband's desk. He always feels the need to confide every little peccadillo to me. He would have told me if he had somehow procured Albert's vowels."

"You think someone planted it in the desk?" George asked.

"Yes. Was it you, Burnley?"

Clearly offended by his mother's accusation, George spluttered his innocence.

Not for the first time, Jacob wondered if he truly wanted to be part of this dysfunctional family. The answer, of course, was that he loved Jane too much to walk away. "If I may make a suggestion, my lady," he said to the Countess, deeming it wiser to wait for her reaction before explaining himself.

"Well?" she demanded, tapping one foot impatiently.

"I've been assisting the inspector with his enquiries." His assertion was somewhat wide of the mark, but she didn't know that.

"And?"

"He might be willing to tell me who informed him about the note in the desk."

"What did you say your name was?"

"Jacob Longworth, my lady."

"Very well, Longworth. See to it."

"Wait a moment," George shouted when his mother turned to leave.

"What is it?" she hissed.

"I just remembered. The constable said Uncle Clarence told the police about the note in Papa's desk."

The color drained from the countess's face. "You're a liar," she retorted, before exiting in a huff.

Chapter 26

Extortion

Preoccupied with the worrisome events that had taken place the previous day, Jacob arrived at the brewery later than his usual crack-of-dawn arrival. Jenkinson and his crew were already hard at work, their distant voices echoing off the brick walls. Upon entering his office, Jacob noticed a small manila envelope on his desk. Curious, he slit it open and extracted a single piece of paper. His knees threatened to buckle as he read the contents of the unsigned, hand-written letter.

> *Longworth,*
> *Five thousand pounds by the end of the week or we take over the brewery.*
> *If you continue your pursuit of Lady Jane Yate, you'll forfeit more than your brewery.*

The monetary threat was gut-wrenching enough, but give up Jane? Never!

Pondering his next move, he sought out Jenkinson. "Did you see who delivered this envelope to my office?" he asked.

"Nay, I've bin in t'other part o' brewery, but Billy's bin groomin' Daisy since early morn. He dotes on that 'oss."

Jacob hurried to the forecourt where Billy was lavishing his usual loving attention on the horse. He asked the same question.

"Aye, a young toff wi' a bit o' a lisp. 'E were right taken wi' Daisy."

Jacob was confused. The Earl had been released on his own recognizance the previous evening, but he couldn't be described as a young toff. For that matter, neither could Clarence Yate. Jacob had thought they were close to solving the mystery, but a new suspect had arrived on the scene.

JACOB'S NOTE WAS BRIEF. He'd received a demand letter. That news alone was enough to prompt Jane into hurrying to the brewery.

Upon arrival, she learned of the entire malicious extent of the letter, and that the person who'd delivered it spoke with a lisp. "It must have been my cousin, Frederick," she exclaimed. "I might have known he'd be mixed up in this. To threaten your life if you continue our relationship is beyond alarming."

Jacob put his arms around her waist. "Never fear," he assured her. "I have no intention of letting you go."

His words were balm to her troubled heart. "I love you," she whispered, as he bent his head to kiss her.

AFTER HEARING from Longworth that he'd received a demand note from the extortionist, Marcus hurried to the brewery.

"Might have known she'd be here," Walsh snarled when they came upon Lady Jane's carriage in the forecourt.

Marcus ignored his constable's predictable sarcasm. All he could think of was that Florence may have accompanied her mistress. As he hoped, he found Lady Jane and her maid in Longworth's office.

"You must see this letter," Lady Jane insisted.

"Why do you suppose we've come?" Walsh sneered in reply.

Florence gasped, clearly outraged.

"That's enough," Marcus said, appalled by his scowling constable's rudeness—to a noblewoman no less. "I apologize," he said, reaching for the letter.

"Short and to the point," Walsh observed, after reading over Marcus's shoulder.

"Looks like this eliminates you as a suspect," Marcus told Longworth.

"Unless he wrote it himself," Walsh replied.

Raking his hair back with both hands, Longworth huffed. "My driver saw the young man who delivered it."

"You could have paid someone," Walsh insisted.

"Answer me this, Constable, if you can," Lady Jane drawled icily. "Why would Mr. Longworth threaten to kill himself if he pursues our friendship?"

Marcus had to hand it to Lady Jane. He supposed she had learned from having six older brothers and an overbearing father not to be intimidated by members of the opposite sex. Walsh wasn't a small man, but she'd put him in his place.

"A ploy, maybe," Walsh muttered, his face as red as a winter beetroot.

Lady Jane ignored him. "From Billy's description, I'd say the young man who delivered the letter could be my cousin, Frederick. He has a pronounced lisp and who else would care if I marry Jacob?"

"Can you explain why you think it might have been your uncle Clarence's son?" Marcus asked.

"Indeed. He's been pestering me to marry him. Perhaps my cousin killed Sharp, and my uncle tried to cover up the crime by shifting suspicion to my father."

ON THE WAY back to Glenairlie with Florrie, Jane realized her relationship with the family's long-serving maid had changed. "Is it because we are both in love that things are different between us?" she asked.

"Perhaps," Florrie allowed. "I admit to feeling like a different person when I'm with Marcus."

"I know exactly what you mean. Jacob arouses feelings I've never experienced before."

"'Tisna only that. Yer family has always treated me well, but Marcus treats me like a person, nay a servant."

"Well, I consider you more than a servant. You're a friend."

"I'll always be a friend to ye, Lady Jane, but I'll ne'er be anything but a servant to yer family. 'Tis the way o' the world."

The rest of the journey passed in silence.

Jane pondered the unfairness of a society her father was bound and determined to preserve, even in the face of the immense changes wrought by the rapid industrialization of Lancashire. He would forbid her marriage to a man he considered inferior simply because he didn't have a title. Frederick matched her in rank and would be deemed suitable to be her husband despite the fact he might be a killer. The possibility made her shudder.

In some ways, Florrie was lucky. She'd fallen in love with a man who was her social equal and would be free to marry him without censure.

Jane resolved to do everything in her power to prove Frederick guilty, then she'd be rid of him for good.

George was exiting the drawing room when Jane arrived home in high dudgeon.

"You won't believe this," she said, before proceeding to tell him about the letter Jacob had received.

"And what makes you think Frederick delivered the letter?" he asked.

"The groomsman described the young man's lisp. It was Frederick."

"We must tell Papa," he replied. "Since being released on his own recognizance, he's been ranting and raving about incompetent policemen."

"Well, the police didn't put that note in his desk. It must have been Frederick."

As expected, their father growled at them when they entered his study, but he listened intently to Jane's explanation of the letter and her belief Frederick delivered it.

"So, my evil twin is trying to protect his son by implicating me," he said. "We'll see about that. We must tell this inspector. What's his name?"

"Halliwell," George replied. "And he already knows."

He escorted his sister from the study.

"What's happening to our family?" she asked tearfully, as she slumped into his embrace.

Distraught over his courageous sister's dismay, George could only shake his head, wishing he'd never met Richard Sharp.

Chapter 27

Parry And Thrust

Filling her lungs, Jane surveyed the men she'd persuaded to gather in Glenairlie's drawing room. Hoping a lifetime of experience dealing with six older brothers would stand her in good stead, she began her well-rehearsed speech. "Now we know Frederick is probably the killer, we must put aside our differences and decide how to entrap him."

"I'm not entirely sure why Caldwell has been invited," George replied haughtily.

Jane resolved to hold on to her patience. "Because, like it or not, he's our half-brother, and has a vested interest in clearing Papa's name."

She was relieved when her response seemed to mollify George's sulk. She couldn't fault his resentment of this newly-discovered half-brother.

"But Halliwell already knows your father didn't send the letter," Jacob offered. "And I'm not all that comfortable being in this house."

Jane had hoped Jacob would be her staunchest ally, but again, his discomfort was understandable.

"Don't worry about that," she replied. "It's highly unlikely our parents will venture into this room."

Philip cleared his throat and raised his hand.

Jane nodded her permission for him to speak, supposing a lifetime of academia had ingrained the habit in him.

"Didn't you say the police only know Frederick delivered the letter? They might assume he was acting for someone else," Philip said.

"Papa, you mean?" Jane replied.

"But how did Uncle Clarence know Albert's IOU was in Papa's desk?" George asked.

"We have to assume our uncle and cousin are both involved," Jane said. "But how do we prove it?"

"I don't understand why they only found my IOU," Albert said. "I thought Sharp held Longworth's vowels too."

"That is puzzling," Jacob agreed.

"Well, I for one am glad the blighter is dead," Francis declared.

"Hear, hear," Victor and Edward chimed in together.

Jane gritted her teeth and prayed for patience. "Yes, that's all well and good. None of us is sorry he's dead, but getting the real killer arrested is of paramount importance."

"I agree," Eliot said. "Jane is right, but surely the police will get the truth out of Frederick."

The men voiced general agreement with this statement. Jane was simply surprised her always taciturn brother had offered it so forcefully. *Half-brother*, she silently reminded herself.

Marcus eyed the squirming young nobleman he was about to interview. Either Frederick Yate had something to hide, or he was intimidated by Walsh standing directly behind him, jaw and fists clenched. "I understand you delivered a letter to Mr. Jacob Longworth at his brewery."

"Wathn't I."

Marcus drummed his fingers on the scarred table between them, then leaned forward. "You spoke to the ostler. We can bring him in to identify you, if you prefer."

"Thew'th no cwime in delivewing a letter."

"There is if it contains a threat of extortion and murder."

"Muwder? Extorthion? No, no, all I did was deliver the letter ath wequethted."

"By whom?"

Frederick shook his head. "You mutht understand that family loyalty ith pawamount to people of my clath."

"Where have we heard that before?" Walsh growled sarcastically. "Answer the question."

Marcus feared Walsh might resort to using his fists, but Frederick finally relented.

"My uncle," he said.

"The Earl?" Marcus asked, needing to be sure.

"Yeth."

A FEW SHORT WEEKS AGO, if anyone had asked where her loyalty lay, Florence wouldn't have hesitated to answer that the Yate family took precedence over all. Now, she struggled with conflicting loyalties. After her fiancé had arrested the Earl, she'd been shunned by the noble family she loved. "The police wouldn't have taken his lordship into custody without proof," she tried, but the furious Countess banished Florence from her presence. Lady Jane's steadfast belief in her father's innocence seemed unshakable. Florence had helped to raise the Yate sons.

Now, they avoided speaking to her, even after the Earl was released on his own recognizance.

She herself believed what she said about the arrest, yet she couldn't conceive of the Earl as a cold-blooded murderer.

Still, Marcus was her future. Heartbroken, she left Glenairlie to seek solace with her beloved.

HAUNTED by the lingering possibility his father had been involved in Richard's death, George barely noticed he was unexpectedly alone in the drawing room with his half-brother. It came to him gradually that Caldwell was the source of heavy sighs and choked coughs. The reality that Philip must be as upset as he was struck him like a blow to the belly.

"I'm not sure what we should do next," Philip said hoarsely.

"Nor I," George admitted.

An uncomfortable silence reigned until Philip said, "No matter what you think of me, I love and respect our father. He has always provided for me, and my mother."

George swallowed the bitterness this revelation caused. "The priority now is to prove Frederick a liar and expose him as the killer."

"I agree, but how?"

George's exasperation increased. "I don't know. Usually, I find practicing swordplay a good way to work out knotty problems."

"Yes, Papa boasted that you're a master swordsman. I suppose that's the reason I took up the practice years ago. I wanted to be as good as you."

Thunderstruck by this news, George asked, "You're proficient with a sword?"

"I can hold my own."

"Against me?"

"Probably not, but I'd try my best."

"Let's find out, shall we?" George replied, hoping his motives were honorable. "A fencing match?"

Fifteen minutes later, they were in Glenairlie's gymnasium, kitted out in protective face guards and padded clothing. The Yate family's fencing master oversaw the proceedings as they crossed tipped epées and began the match.

It took only a few parries and thrusts for George to win, but Philip was nevertheless a worthy opponent. "You just need practice," he told his half-brother, beginning to realize they had more in common than their sexual proclivities. But getting over that stumbling block was for another day.

"I suppose you'll be expected to take on Father's role as earl," Philip said. "At least for the time being."

"No, he won't," echoed off the cement walls.

George's gut clenched when he turned to see his Uncle Clarence had entered the gymnasium.

"The title will rightly fall to *me* when my brother is hanged for his crime."

Chapter 28

Posturing

The team charged with proving the Earl's innocence met again, this time in Jacob's office. In agreement with George that including all the Yate offspring made for an unwieldy group to cram into such a small space, Jane nevertheless insisted on inviting Inspector Halliwell.

George told of Clarence's assertion that he intended to claim the earldom in the event his twin were found guilty and hanged.

Philip corroborated the details.

Jane itched to ask how the pair had ended up fencing in the gymnasium, but resigned herself to being glad the two men who so resembled each other seemed to have something in common at least.

"This puts a new slant on Clarence Yate's information about the IOU in his brother's desk," Halliwell said. "But Frederick was adamant it was the Earl who asked him to deliver the demand letter to Longworth."

"Did my uncle tell you how he knew about the IOU in the desk?" George asked.

"He claimed the Countess told him."

George and Jane snorted their disbelief. "If my father is found guilty," Jane said. "My mother will be shamed. She'd lose her standing in society. As a duke's daughter, she would never do anything to jeopardize her title."

"Even though she once favored Clarence Yate?" Halliwell said discretely.

Jane risked a glance at Philip, surprised he didn't seem shocked. Perhaps their father had told his illegitimate son about his wife's long-ago indiscretion. Their half-brother may have been aware of Eliot's parentage long before she and George learned of it. Looking back on her childhood, Jane recalled too many instances when Eliot had acted spitefully—her other siblings were far from perfect, but she'd always gotten along with them. She couldn't deny that, over the years, she'd subconsciously avoided Eliot. She wondered why it had never occurred to her he was radically different. Did his sly demeanor indicate he knew he wasn't the Earl's son?

Philip's voice dragged her out of her daydream. "If I may," he interjected. "My analysis is this. Uncle and cousin have devised this elaborate plot to discredit the Earl, so that Clarence may claim the title for himself."

Murdering Richard Sharp in order to lay claim to the title seemed far-fetched and convoluted to Jane, but Philip supposedly had the analytical brain of an academic.

As the meeting wound down, Marcus took Viscount Burnley aside. "My lord," he began. "It's imperative we establish once and for all your mother's role in this."

"I agree, but I suggest we take Jane with us to confront her."

Lady Jane was reluctant but finally saw the necessity of

finding out if the Countess did, in fact, tell Clarence Yate about the IOU in the Earl's desk, as he claimed.

Based on his last interaction with the Countess of Leyland, Marcus expected a heated encounter when they arrived at Glenairlie, but once they convinced the gatekeeper to allow them entry, he was surprised that the noblewoman's animosity seemed to be directed as much at her eldest son as at him. Only Lady Jane's calm demeanor softened her vitriol, and she agreed to answer a few questions.

Marcus cleared his throat. "My lady, did you, or did you not, tell Lord Clarence Yate about Albert's IOU in your husband's desk?"

"Why would I do such a thing?" she replied. "As if I am privy to the contents of my husband's desk."

Marcus filled his lungs. "Please answer the question, Your Ladyship."

The Countess snorted. "Had I married a duke, you'd be addressing me as Your Grace."

"Mama," the viscount interjected. "Stop this posturing and answer truthfully. Papa's life may depend on it."

The Countess pouted. "Of course I didn't tell Clarence anything of the sort. He's a liar if he claimed I did."

Marcus could draw only one conclusion. Lord Clarence Yate had planted the incriminating evidence. It followed then that he and Frederick were lying about the Earl's involvement.

As the trio turned to leave, Lady Jane hesitated. "One last question, if I may, Mama," she said softly, slumping to her knees in front of her mother. "Does Eliot know he is Uncle Clarence's son?"

GEORGE'S HEART broke for his little sister. As the only girl in the family, she should have enjoyed the love of a doting mother. Yet, even now as Jane more or less begged for affection and truth, the Countess's shoulders remained stiff and she avoided her only daughter's gaze.

"I have never told him."

Startled by his mother's honesty, George felt nothing but pity for this unhappy woman who had brought him into the world.

Jane persisted. "But does Eliot know?"

"The Earl may have told him out of spite. Or Sharp?"

"Might Uncle Clarence have told him?" George asked.

"Possibly. I have done my utmost to shield my son from the truth. He and I have never discussed it."

Looking back on a lifetime of parental neglect, George realized his mother had always considered Eliot her only son. Thinking now about his often testy relationship with Eliot, he knew for certain that his half-brother was aware of the truth.

WHEN JANE RETURNED to the brewery after confronting her mother, she was understandably upset. Jacob regretted her grief, but was elated she'd turned to him for solace. "Let me take you home to Deane," he suggested, looking forward to an evening of cuddling and intimate touching.

He sensed her hesitation. "Will you not let me kiss away the hurts?"

"Something is bothering me about recent revelations," she replied. "I need to confront Eliot and find out the truth once and for all."

"But we've established your uncle and cousin are the killers. How will speaking with Eliot change any of that?"

"I don't know," she admitted. "Perhaps it's the last family secret I need to expose. Then I can make a clean break with my parents."

"You're sure about this?" he asked. "Life with me won't be the same, you know."

"If they can't accept you after all I've learned about their duplicity, then I'll be happier with you."

"Come home with me now," he urged, afraid she might change her mind if she returned to Glenairlie. "You can confront Eliot on the morrow."

"No. It has to be tonight. Then you and I can be free of the secrets."

He couldn't explain the sense of dread welling up in his throat. "Let me come with you."

She shook her head. "I have to do this alone. Eliot's more likely to tell the truth if he doesn't feel backed into a corner."

He took her into his embrace and kissed her goodbye, unable to shake the feeling of doom gripping his heart.

BACK AT GLENAIRLIE, Jane fumed. Her plan to speak with Eliot had come to naught. He'd refused to open the bedroom door in response to her entreaties. "Unbelievable," she exclaimed to George when she joined him in the drawing room. "He told me to go away."

"He's always been stubborn," he replied.

"And rude."

It struck Jane more forcefully than ever that, apart from George, she didn't know her brothers well at all. "Thank goodness I have you as a brother," she told him.

Chapter 29

Fisticuffs

Florence struggled with conflicting emotions. Brought up in the Presbyterian faith, she knew it was wrong to cohabit with a man, but she couldn't bring herself to return to the censure that awaited her at Glenairlie.

Her presence in Marcus's flat made life difficult for them both. She knew enough about men's physical needs to realize that living at close quarters with only one small bed was torture for her fiancé. It was also hard for her to resist the temptations of the flesh. In addition, members of the police force were expected to maintain high standards in their personal lives. She and Marcus weren't *living in sin*, but the gossips would spread the word that they were.

Therefore, the news from Marcus that Clarence and Frederick Yate were to be charged with the murder came as a huge relief. She only hoped the Yate family would forgive the role they perceived she'd played in the Earl's arrest. She missed them all dearly, but especially Lady Jane. She was a commoner, but the noble Yates were the only family she'd known for ten years. It struck her as ironic that ten years was exactly the same length of time Marcus had pined for his dead Eliza. Perhaps their emergence into a new life together was meant to be. Her Scottish grannie would certainly agree—a memory that conjured a smile.

In all the years she'd worked for the Yates, she'd never given her homeland much thought. Now, a wave of nostalgia washed over her, and she wondered if Marcus would be willing to travel to Edinburgh after their marriage. Grannie was long since gone, but she'd have loved Marcus—a kind, considerate man who was good at his job, which was more than could be said for his constable. Walsh struck her as a man with a perpetual chip on his shoulder, though she'd never heard Marcus utter a word against him.

Marcus agreed to accompany Florence when she returned to Glenairlie. They held hands in the hackney and he sensed her nervousness. Findley had reported that the Earl had accepted the police force's apology for his wrongful arrest with good grace, but there was no telling what his or the family's reaction would be to Florence's return. "We'll work something out if they refuse to take you back," he said in an effort to allay her fears.

"I ken ye willna see me homeless," she replied. "But they're ma family."

"I understand, but you and I are destined to create a new family of our own."

"Speakin' o' family, would ye be willin' to visit Edinburgh once we're wed?"

Marcus chuckled. Florence wanted her Scottish relatives to meet him. "A honeymoon of sorts, you mean?"

"Aye, 'tis ten..."

The hackney had come to a halt in front of Glenairlie, but

the fisticuffs taking place on the front steps stunned Florence to silence.

Marcus leaped from the cab and ran to pull Frederick Yate off another young man he seemed intent on thrashing. Lady Jane was screaming at both men to stop fighting. It appeared the youth Marcus didn't recognize was Eliot Yate.

Viscount Burnley arrived and helped Marcus separate the two combatants.

Restrained, both continued to hurl verbal abuse at each other.

"What's going on here?" Burnley demanded.

"Athk him," Frederick retorted.

"He attacked me for no reason," Eliot countered.

"I had good weathons."

Believing the fight had gone out of Frederick, Marcus loosened his grip. "Want to enlighten us as to what this is all about?" he asked, sensing the altercation had some bearing on the investigation.

"Thertainly, Inspector," he replied, shrugging free of the restraint. "I want to change my thtatement."

GEORGE HAD NEVER BEEN OVERLY-FOND of any of his male siblings. They lacked maturity. Eliot was a different kettle of fish. He'd always struck George as too secretive, too sly. Admittedly, discovering Eliot's true parentage had done nothing to improve his opinion. He didn't particularly care for Frederick either. Perhaps the fact Eliot and Frederick were both Clarence's sons had something to do with it. There was an inherent untrustworthiness about both young men. He wondered if each was aware the other was his half-brother. Is that what the fight had been about?

"Settle down," he told Eliot when the lad struggled to be free of his grip. "Papa's had enough upset."

"He's not my papa," Eliot hissed in reply, finally breaking free.

George set off in pursuit. "Well, that answers one question," he muttered as he mounted the stairs to his brother's room. When Eliot slammed the door in his face, he barged in before the lad had a chance to refuse him entry.

About to unleash a string of recriminations, he paused, puzzled by the guilty look on Eliot's face and his hasty attempt to push something under his pillow. "Want to explain?"

"No. Go away."

"Look, I understand the recent revelations about…"

Eliot glared, his split lip twisted into a grimace. "You think you know everything because you'll inherit the earldom. Well, think again. You understand nothing. Leave me alone."

Sometimes, retreat was the best option if a man wanted to gain ground another day. With a heavy heart, George left the bedroom and closed the door behind him with a firm click.

Frustrated that Eliot had steadfastly refused to open the door to her entreaties the previous evening, and flustered by the fight and the vitriol that had spewed forth from both combatants, Jane suddenly realized Florrie had come home. She couldn't hold back the tears as she ran to hug her maid. "Thank goodness you've returned," she exclaimed. "Glenairlie just hasn't been the same without you."

"And how is yer father?" Florrie asked, dabbing Jane's tears with a hankie.

"Good, except he's furious about Uncle Clarence and Frederick, of course."

"So, he doesna blame my Marcus, or me?"

"No. If we made you feel that way, I'm sorry. We were all in a state of shock."

"Aye."

Having retrieved his stovepipe hat from the ground, Halliwell joined them.

"I was just apologizing to Florrie," Jane said. "We owe you an apology too. You were simply doing your job."

"This has been a difficult case," the policeman allowed. "Lots of twists and turns. Now, your cousin wants to change his statement. I told him to meet me at the station, so I'll leave Florence with you."

"She'll be safe with me, but what do you suppose the fight was all about?"

"I hope to learn that from Frederick."

Chapter 30

Interrogation

"He's angry," Walsh told Marcus as they prepared to question Frederick Yate for the second time.

"Angry doesn't begin to describe how he behaved during the fight outside Glenairlie. He was downright livid."

"Looks like he still is. The black eye doesn't help."

Anxious to hear what had riled the young nobleman, Marcus nodded. "Let's get it over with."

Frederick squared his shoulders when they entered the cubicle and declared, "I with to amend my pweviouth thtatement."

"So you said. Explain."

"It wathn't my uncle who gave me the letter."

"Who was it?"

"My father."

Marcus was puzzled. "So, what has brought on this change of heart?"

"Papa convinthed me my uncle wath the killer. I assumed I would be named Viscount Burnley if my father became the Earl of Leyland."

"In other words, you'd be next in line to inherit."

"However, it theems I wath wong. Appawently, I have an older bwother who'll inhewit."

Marcus wasn't surprised when Walsh fisted his hands. The constable probably itched to thump the affected lisp out of the whining brat. However, the reason for the fight had suddenly become obvious. Frederick hadn't known about Eliot.

"So, is it your belief that your father killed Richard Sharp in order to frame the Earl?"

The anger drained from Frederick's face. "Thteady on, old chap. I nevew thaid Papa wath the murdewer. Ath far ath I know, he doethn't even have the vowels."

"Nevertheless," Marcus replied, tired of the games the Yates were playing. "We'll have to bring him in for questioning."

Thanks largely to the servants' rumor mill, news of the fight in the grounds of Glenairlie soon spread beyond the confines of upper-class Heaton. Word reached Jacob's housekeeper in Deane that Frederick Yate intended to change the statement he'd given to police. The loyal Mrs. Banks immediately informed Jacob. Perplexed by what this meant for him personally, Jacob hurried to the police station to see Inspector Halliwell.

He arrived just in time to see Jane's cousin boarding a hackney.

"What has he said?" he asked the Inspector when he tracked him down inside.

"That his father gave him the demand letter to give to you."

Relieved to learn Jane's father was no longer a suspect, Jacob asked, "So, Lady Jane's uncle has my vowels."

"Young Frederick didn't seem to think so."

"I don't understand. Why send me the letter if he doesn't have the IOUs?"

"And why demand you stop seeing Lady Jane?" Walsh asked.

"Perhaps the plan was for Frederick to marry Lady Jane," Marcus suggested.

Frustrated, Jacob scratched his head. "If Clarence Yate doesn't have the vowels, then who does?"

"That's the most intriguing question," Halliwell declared. "One we definitely need to put to Lord Clarence Yate—when we find him."

"I'LL SAY ONE THING," Jane told Florrie a week later. "This ordeal has had an unexpected effect on Papa."

"I've noticed he doesna shout as much," her maid replied.

"It seems strange not to hear his voice bellowing from his study."

"And he hasna objected to yer young man's occasional visits."

Jane hoped her father's softened demeanor augured well for the future. "He's been strangely quiet about Uncle Clarence's arrest in Manchester."

"Aye. And he said naught about it takin' a verra nerve-wrackin' week to track him down."

"I just hope he's not a simmering volcano that will blow its top when we least expect it."

"I suppose it depends what secrets emerge from Lord Clarence when he finally speaks. 'Tisna surpisin' the Countess has been even more reclusive than usual."

"Eliot too for that matter," Jane replied, suddenly realizing she hadn't seen her half-brother since the altercation with Frederick. "He must feel like an outcast, given all that's transpired. We need to repair the damage done to our family. Eliot and I have never been close but we must make an effort to preserve family unity."

"What do ye ha'e in mind?"

"I should try to talk to him."

"Good luck. Eliot has ne'er bin the talkative sort."

"Yes. I murdered Richard Sharp," Lord Clarence Yate declared. "Lock me up and throw away the key."

Marcus exchanged a glance with Walsh and saw the same doubt in the constable's eyes. The nobleman wasn't telling the whole story. "Can you tell us what happened?"

"I'd rather not."

"It might go better for you if we know the details."

Hampered by handcuffs, Yate tried unsuccessfully to fold his arms. "Well, it was an accident."

Marcus arched a brow. "You argued, a pushing match ensued, he fell into the mash tun."

"Exactly so."

"What did you argue about?" Walsh asked.

"Er…this and that."

"About the fact you're Eliot's father?" Marcus suggested.

Yate clenched his jaw. "Yes."

"And you didn't try to pull Sharp out of the mash tun?"

"No. He was screaming so loudly, I'm ashamed to say I panicked and ran."

"So, you didn't remove anything from Sharp's pockets?"

"Good grief, do you take me for a pickpocket?"

Walsh rolled his eyes.

"We'll write up a statement and get you to sign it later,"

Marcus explained, realizing it was pointless to continue. "For now, you'll be escorted back to your cell."

He and Walsh held their peace until a guard had removed the shackled nobleman. Then, both shook their heads.

"He's not the killer," Marcus sighed. He'd harbored high hopes of being free to give his full attention to his upcoming nuptials.

Walsh nodded his agreement. "No mention of the hammer blow and he had no clue about the missing IOUs."

"Plus, the brewery workers didn't report any screaming."

"Sharp could hardly scream if his head had been caved in."

"Right. Clarence Yate is protecting someone," Marcus said, reluctant to admit they hadn't yet found the real culprit.

"I KEEP GOING over what Eliot said after the fight with Frederick," George told Jane. "It bothers me and I don't feel good about your approaching him."

"Tell me exactly what he said," she replied.

"In the courtyard, he revealed he knew Papa isn't his father."

"Yes, I heard that."

"Upstairs, he said, 'You think you know everything because you'll inherit the earldom. Well, think again. You understand nothing. Leave me alone.'"

Jane frowned. "Perhaps he was simply lashing out because he was upset by the fight. Frederick got in a few nasty punches."

"It wasn't just what he said. He was hiding something."

"But he already revealed he knew of his parentage."

"No, I mean literally hiding. I entered rather abruptly when he slammed the door in my face. He had a guilty look on his face and I got the feeling he was trying to conceal something under his pillow."

"Well, maybe I'll ask him what it was."

George had his doubts. "I haven't seen him since that day, but I hope he's cooled off."

Jane smiled. "Don't worry. Admit it. All my brothers love me. I'll get him to open up."

George wished he shared his sister's confidence.

Chapter 31

Could It Be?

Determined to have it out with Eliot once and for all, Jane was startled by the announcement of Jacob's unexpected arrival at Glenairlie.

"You've told me your father's demeanor has changed," he told her, as she ushered him into the drawing room. "So, perhaps this is a perfect time to ask for your hand."

She was delighted he'd taken the bull by the horns, so to speak, and could hardly tell him she wanted to rush off to speak to Eliot. "I love you for it," she said. "But even if Papa agrees, Mama will be a different story."

"Nevertheless, I'm here now."

He was so close, it was impossible not to touch him. He drew her like a lodestone. When she touched his tempting lips, he took hold of her wrist and gently nibbled her fingertips, all the while gazing knowingly into her eyes.

"I'm tempted to invite you upstairs to my bedroom," she whispered.

"That would be hard to resist," he replied. "But then your father would send me packing with a rifle."

"I suppose you're right," she sighed, taking his hand. "Come with me."

She led him to the study, strangely bothered by the lack of loud voices. She even hesitated after tapping on the door, something she never did.

"Don't be nervous," Jacob whispered. "Whatever happens we will be together, I promise."

"Enter," her father intoned. "Jane," he exclaimed when she and Jacob entered. "It's not like you to wait to be invited."

"No, Papa," she replied meekly.

Her father eyed Jacob. "The answer is no."

"You haven't heard my proposition," Jacob retorted angrily.

"You want to marry my daughter."

"I do. I love her and promise to cherish her all my life."

The earl snorted. "I forbid it. You're a commoner, a brewery owner."

"I may not be of noble blood, but I know how to act honorably. My family's stellar reputation as honest and successful tradesmen is well-known."

Jane cringed. Could Jacob have made his disgust of recent goings-on any plainer?

Her father narrowed his eyes. "Point taken," he allowed. "What about these debts of yours?"

"My original lenders arranged for a ten-year repayment plan and I was honoring that schedule comfortably. It was Richard Sharp who tried to extort the full amount in a week."

"And now he's dead."

"Not by my hand."

"Nor mine," her father replied with a chuckle.

"Please, Papa, won't you consider Jacob's suit? I love him."

Her father stroked his beard for long, interminable minutes. All Jane heard was the loud ticking of the clock on the credenza, until he said, "Once the matter of the missing IOUs is settled, then we'll talk again, young man."

He dismissed them with a wave of his hand.

Jane pecked a kiss on his cheek and left feeling giddily optimistic.

Jᴀᴄᴏʙ ᴡɪꜱʜᴇᴅ he felt as optimistic as Jane. "I suppose that went well," was all he could manage, anxious not to ruin her good humor.

"Better than I expected," she admitted.

"But this matter of the missing vowels still stands in the way of our happiness."

"Don't you think though," she replied. "If someone actually produces the IOUs, they are practically admitting they killed Sharp?"

"We thought that about your uncle, but Halliwell informs me that isn't the case."

"What?"

"The police don't think he is the murderer. He confessed but couldn't provide the correct details about the crime, and he doesn't have the vowels."

"Perhaps he hid them somewhere."

"Apparently he was outraged when Halliwell asked him if he'd removed anything from Sharp's pockets."

"He confessed to being a murderer, but balked at the suggestion he's a thief?"

"That's about the size of it."

"He's always been a sly devil."

"Halliwell thinks he is protecting someone else."

"That can only be Frederick," she replied.

"Or Eliot."

Jacob's comment about Eliot unsettled Jane long after he'd left reluctantly, citing a pressing delivery of beer for a local ale house.

A short time ago, she'd have dismissed the suggestion that her half-brother was involved in a murder as ludicrous, but since then, she'd discovered things about Eliot she hadn't been aware of.

Did she really know him? She and George had always been close—the eldest and the youngest. Her other brothers—well, they were young men who still behaved like little boys. She'd never really befriended any of them, deeming them jealous of the extra consideration her father gave her. She would be the first to admit she got away with a lot more transgressions than they did, but it was natural for a father to spoil his only daughter.

However, now she knew Eliot wasn't Papa's son, it didn't make sense that he would be jealous of her relationship with her father.

She had reached his door when she suddenly recalled what George had said about Eliot trying to hide something under his pillow. Her heart lurched. Could it be...?

Her intention to speak to Eliot in order to mend fences took on a whole new dimension. She'd have to search his room in order to be sure he didn't have Jacob's vowels. That was easier said than done since he hadn't left his bedroom for days. She could think of only one person who might dislodge him from his hibernation.

Prepared for a frosty reception, she tiptoed further along the landing, inhaled deeply, and tapped on her mother's door. She'd never been able to wheedle concessions out of the Countess of Leyland.

Experience taught her to wait for permission before she entered.

"What do you want?" her sullen mother asked after Ethel allowed her entry.

Keeping the smile plastered on her face, Jane replied, "I'm worried about Eliot."

"Concerned for someone other than yourself. That's a first."

Ignoring the sarcasm, Jane continued. "Now, Mama, I know you must be worried too. He hasn't left his room in days. What do you think is bothering him?"

"You are aware he's your half-brother?"

"That makes no difference to me," she replied, wishing it were true. "Has he always known?"

"I'm not sure."

Jane pitied the obvious sadness in her mother's reply, so she took a chance. "Do you think it would it help if you talked about it with him?"

The countess narrowed her eyes, but then she nodded. "Perhaps you're right. But how do we get him to come to my suite?"

Dismayed by her own deviousness, Jane replied, "Pen a note and I'll slip it under his door."

Chapter 32

Good News And Bad

George paused in the shadows when he saw Eliot exit his bedroom, move cautiously along the hall, and tap on his mother's door. He'd always been her favorite, and George now understood the reason. At least the boy had come out of hiding.

He was about to continue on his way when Jane appeared. She tried Eliot's door, grimacing when it refused to open.

"He's gone to Mama's suite," he said, sorry he'd startled her when she squealed.

"You frightened me," she replied, clutching her throat. "I know he's not there."

He narrowed his eyes. "What are you up to, young lady?"

"I simply want to find out what he's hiding."

"You think he has the vowels."

"Don't you?"

"It crossed my mind."

"But it won't open. I think he locked it."

"Step aside. Your room is upstairs. All our brothers have rooms on this floor and none of them lock. But they do tend to stick."

He put his shoulder to the door and lifted as he pushed and turned the knob.

"You did it," she whispered when the door opened. "Keep watch."

"Hurry up."

Jane didn't need to be told twice. There was no guarantee Eliot would wish to prolong a heart-to-heart chat with his mother.

Doubting whatever he'd hidden was still under his pillow, she began with the bedside tables. They yielded nothing untoward, nor did the wardrobe, nor the desk.

Exasperated and getting more nervous by the second, she lifted the pillow of the unmade bed.

Eureka!

She scanned the documents. The names of Jacob's original lenders had been scratched out and replaced with Richard Sharp's name. A line had been drawn through Sharp's name, but no one else's name had been written in instead.

"What do you make of this?" she asked George after exiting the bedroom.

"We need to confront him," her brother declared after quickly perusing the documents.

"Not now. I'm going to get them into Jacob's hands right away," she replied, startling when the door to her mother's suite opened and Eliot emerged.

He hesitated, narrowing his eyes when he saw them.

"Eliot," George acknowledged with a nod as he took Jane's arm and quickly escorted her down the stairs.

"Do you think he suspects?" she asked when they reached the foyer.

"Difficult to say," he replied. "I've always found him hard to read."

JACOB HAD JUST FINISHED HELPING to load the wagon when an unexpected visitor entered the yard. He'd always had a lot of respect for Martin Eccleston—until the banker sold his note to Sharp.

"I'm surprised to see you here," Jacob said, slightly amused that Eccleston looked angry. If anyone had a right to be upset...

Eccleston cleared his throat. "You've missed a payment, Longworth. It's not like you to default, so I came to ascertain the problem."

"I beg your pardon?" Jacob replied as he jumped down from the wagon.

"The payment was due on the tenth as usual. You didn't make it. I understand from Cruikshank and Walters that you haven't paid them either. You are aware we are entitled to call the loans if..."

"Hold on," Jacob retorted. "Are you telling me you didn't sell my vowels to Richard Sharp?"

"Richard who?"

"Sharp."

"Why would we sell good investments to someone we've never heard of?"

Eccleston listened while Jacob explained recent happenings. "So, you thought..."

Jacob combed his fingers through his hair as the knot in his belly gradually unwound. "Yes. You'll receive the payments by tomorrow at the latest."

"Good. I'll inform the others. This Sharp fellow was murdered, you say?"

"Right here, in my brewery."

"And the police haven't arrested anyone?"

"Inspector Halliwell has had a couple of people in custody, but they've turned out to be innocent."

"Halliwell? Good man. Don't you worry. He'll track down the killer."

Suddenly, Jacob didn't care if they caught the murderer or not. An enormous weight had been lifted from his shoulders. He might now have a chance to convince the Earl of his suitability. He left his men to finish loading the wagon. "As soon as everything is loaded," he shouted to Billy. "You can make the delivery to *The Lion*."

"Right-o," Billy replied.

Anxious to tell Jane the good news, Jacob jumped into his carriage and directed Henry to Glenairlie.

JANE'S CARRIAGE almost collided with the beer wagon that Daisy was pulling out of the brewery yard. She leaned out the window to learn the reason for her driver's curses.

"Sorry, Lady Jane," Billy shouted as he reined in the horse. "If tha's lookin' fer Master Jacob, he left; told his driver to teck him to Glenairlie."

"Botheration," she cried. "I brought good news."

"Seemed in good spirits hisself. There's another young man waitin' fer 'im int' office."

"A young man?"

"Aye."

Jane's blood ran cold. Common sense told her to stay in the carriage and head for home, but the dread knotting her belly urged her to investigate. If it wasn't Eliot in the office, she could come up with some flippant excuse, retreat quickly and warn

Jacob. If Eliot was there—she didn't know precisely what she would do, but there had to be a way to solve this horrible situation. Reason convinced her it couldn't be Eliot. He'd been at home when she left.

Billy resumed his journey while her driver helped her alight from the carriage. "I won't be long," she told him. "Wait here in the street." She squared her shoulders, swallowed her fear and marched into the brewery.

Her throat constricted and her legs trembled when she encountered Eliot in Jacob's office. Evil lurked in his narrowed eyes. "Why?" was all she could think to ask as her knees threatened to buckle. But she couldn't allow him to see her fear.

"Sharp threatened Mama," he hissed.

"But..."

"I followed him here, demanded he stop persecuting her."

"But..."

"He just laughed then picked up a hammer someone had left lying about."

"He had the hammer?"

"I ran, like a coward."

Jane was beginning to understand. "You ran up the ladder."

"It was a mistake. He cornered me. I could see the evil glint in his eyes when he espied the steaming malt in the tun."

"Oh, Eliot, you must have been terrified."

"I was, until he made the mistake of chucking the hammer at me. I caught it and took a swing as he approached. I missed, but a noise from below snagged his attention and I swung again. He dropped like a stone."

"Into the tun."

"No. I rifled through his pockets, then hefted him into the tun. Bloody heavy, I can tell you."

He admitted it so casually, a shiver stole up Jane's spine. "But it was self-defense," she tried. "If you give yourself up..."

"You're naive, Sis," he growled, as he rose from the chair and lunged for her.

She squealed and turned to run, but he caught hold of her hair and forced her to her knees. "What are you doing?" she gasped, as pain arrowed into her scalp.

He grabbed her reticule with his free hand. "You're going to give me the documents you stole from my room and then I'll decide what to do with you."

She was glad she'd secreted the vowels on her person. Surely he wouldn't dare put his hands on her.

She closed her eyes and swallowed her shock when he tore the front of her bodice to reveal the hidden IOUs. The chain of her pendant snapped, sending Jacob's precious ruby tumbling to the floor.

Tempted to sob, she decided not to give him the satisfaction of seeing her fear as he bound her wrists and tied a gag over her mouth. He dragged her out of the office, then across the cobble-stones of the yard, where he shoved her into the stable and covered her with hay. "I'll let the horse deal with you," he hissed, as he latched the door and made his escape.

Struggling to breathe, she lay cocooned in the damp straw and wept desperate tears.

Chapter 33

Crushing Weight

Jacob's optimism faltered when Viscount Burnley and Inspector Halliwell hastened out of Glenairlie to greet his carriage.

"Is Lady Jane not with you?" the policeman asked when Jacob stepped down from the carriage.

"I haven't seen her," he replied. "I came to tell her the good news."

"Good news?" Burnley asked.

"Sharp lied about buying my vowels. The original lenders still hold the notes."

"That is good news," George replied. "But we're concerned you two didn't cross paths. Jane found your vowels in Eliot's room. She set off posthaste to get them into your hands."

Jacob knew the vowels couldn't be the originals, but something George had said caught his attention. "Eliot is involved?"

Burnley nodded. "So it would seem, I'm sorry to say."

"Where is he now? I'd like to give him a piece of my mind."

"That's what worries us," Halliwell explained. "He's not in the house and his horse is missing. The viscount sent me a note when he became concerned."

A lead weight settled in Jacob's belly. "You think he's gone after her."

In reply, George shoved Jacob back into the carriage. Halliwell climbed aboard hastily and ordered the driver to take them to the brewery.

"I'll kill him if he hurts her," Jacob hissed.

"I'll help," George promised between gritted teeth.

The inspector remained silent, his jaw firmly clenched.

AS THE CARRIAGE HURTLED ALONG, George grappled with the probability that his half-brother had killed Richard Sharp.

His emotions were mixed. He'd loved Richard, but hated the misery he'd inflicted on the Yate family and others. Try as he might, he couldn't conceive of a reason for Eliot to murder Richard. Guilt fogged his brain. Perhaps if he hadn't indulged his lover, things might have been different. Evidently, Richard hadn't used his money to buy up vowels, so clearly, he'd squandered it on something else.

George had always boasted he was a good judge of character, but...

One thing was for certain—he would never trust his heart to anyone again. His forbidden infatuation had led to nothing but grief.

He was tempted to apologize to Longworth for the part he'd played in the disastrous affair, but that would mean laying bare his biggest secret, and the brewer was obviously frantically preoccupied with making sure Jane was safe. Nor could he come clean with the policeman present.

"My sister is lucky to have found you, Longworth," was all he could manage to growl from his parched throat.

Marcus fully understood Longworth's agony. He'd be just as frantically worried if he thought Florence's life was threatened. Burnley's anxiety was also understandable, though Marcus got the feeling the viscount was keeping something to himself. However, aristocrats were famous for not allowing their emotions to show.

He pondered the whole complicated business of solving murders. He had to admit that the first two cases he'd been assigned to—the beating death of a boy at Broadclough Mills and the garroting of Fred Chadwick at *The Hippodrome Music Hall*—had been solved quite by chance, and not necessarily thanks to his efforts.

As for the murder of Richard Sharp, he'd never even considered young Eliot Yate as a suspect, hadn't really thought of his involvement. Yet, it appeared the chap had committed the murder and was now threatening his sister.

Despite delving as far as he was allowed into the Yate family's activities, Marcus again got the feeling there was too much about the family he hadn't uncovered. Too many skeletons in too many cupboards! He'd known from the outset that dealing with an aristocratic family would be challenging.

If Walsh were present, he'd no doubt have many negative comments to offer about aristocrats.

Fear, exhaustion, and the reek of horse manure lulled Jane into a fitful sleep. Having managed to ascertain that the stall was tiny for a big dray horse, she knew she'd be crushed under Daisy's huge hooves. Or if the horse rolled over on her... Did horses sleep standing up or did they...

Startled from her reverie by the unmistakable sound of the beer wagon returning, she tried to shout, but the gag prevented her from alerting Billy to her presence.

She wriggled all the more desperately when she heard a carriage arrive, then frantic voices, Jacob's among them. Her throat constricted when they grew fainter. They'd gone into the brewery. She'd be dead before they found her.

Praying death would come quickly, she closed her tear-filled eyes and sent a silent message to the man she loved. "Goodbye, Jacob, my heart."

JACOB PRAYED he'd find Jane safe and sound in his office, but his hopes were cruelly dashed. There was no sign of her. His first terrifying fear was that Eliot might have shoved her into the mash tun.

"Up there," he growled, pointing to the platform.

Climbing the ladder had always been a chore. Now, his feet flew. Sobbing with relief, he fell to his knees when he discovered there was no boiled body floating in the mash tun.

George had followed him. "Where else could he have taken her?" he demanded, his reassuring hand pressed to Jacob's shoulder.

"You tell me," he replied. "He's your fyking brother."

Instantly regretting his outburst, he apologized and started back down the ladder.

Halliwell had remained on the brewery floor. "Let's go back to your office and think about this calmly," he suggested.

His belly in knots, Jacob preferred to be out searching but he agreed they should confer as to the best course of action. He slumped down in his office chair and leaned forward, his head in his hands. Barely aware of the others' voices, he noticed something red and shiny on the floor beneath his desk.

"Jane's ruby," he exclaimed, his heart careening around his ribcage as he held the gem aloft.

His euphoria was short-lived when he realized the chain had been broken. The pendant had been torn from Jane's body.

Jane tried to scream when the door to the stall creaked open.

"In tha goes, Daisy lass," Billy urged.

Jane squeezed her eyes tight shut and waited for the weight of a heavy hoof to crush her body.

"What ails thee, Daisy?" Billy asked. "Go on."

Jane risked opening her eyes and found herself looking into the wise gaze of the big horse.

Daisy knew she was there and was refusing to enter the stall. A fragile hope blossomed in her heart.

From the huffing and puffing, she guessed Billy was trying to shove the horse from the rear, but Daisy snorted and shook her head.

Jane willed the horse to stand her ground.

"By gum, lass," Billy shouted, clearly agitated. "Tha's a stubborn bugger. I need t'kip if tha doesna."

"What now?" George exclaimed with exasperation when noise of a commotion going on in the yard reached their ears.

"That's just Billy," Jacob replied, too heartsick to investigate. "Sounds like he's having trouble with Daisy."

Halliwell frowned. "Is that normal?" he asked.

Suddenly alert, Jacob sat up straight. "No, it's not."

Clutching the ruby, he sprang from the chair and hurried into the yard.

Mopping his brow, Billy had his back to Daisy's rump and was trying to shove her into the stall.

"Don't know what's come o'er her," he told the three newcomers when he saw them.

Jacob knew instantly. "Jane's in there," he yelled, rushing into the stall as fast as his legs would carry him. "Hold Daisy."

Falling to his knees, he dug frantically into the piles of hay, unable to hold back a sob when he finally looked into Jane's tear-filled eyes. He swore to kill the wretch who'd bound and gagged her and left her to die. "You're safe now," he said softly as he removed the gag.

Jaw clenched as he stared at his sister's ruined bodice, George knelt beside him, produced a sheathed dagger from an inside pocket and cut the rope binding her hands.

Jacob scooped her up and cradled her in his arms as she sobbed. "He'll never hurt you again, I promise," he whispered.

"Tha's a champion, all reet," Billy crooned to the nodding horse.

Chapter 34

Moot

Longworth wanted to take Lady Jane straight to Deane. After he carried her into his house, the inspector directed the driver to the police station. George agreed it might be advisable to have Constable Walsh accompany him and Halliwell to Glenairlie, but the delay only added to his frustration. "I'm fairly certain Eliot will have fled to his mother," he told the inspector. "Our best chance is to nab him quickly before Mama spirits him to safety."

"You think she'll try to protect him?" the inspector asked.

"There's no doubt in my mind," Burnley replied. "And Papa will help her."

"Why?" Halliwell asked. "Eliot isn't his son."

"No, but my parents will close ranks to protect their good name."

"Lady Jane fell unusually quiet cradled in Longworth's arms, but I fear she will have something to say about that when she recovers from her ordeal."

"Exactly," Burnley replied. "Furthermore, Uncle Clarence will do what he deems necessary to protect Eliot."

Halliwell agreed. "He already confessed to a murder he didn't commit for his son's sake."

As the carriage approached Glenairlie, the policeman voiced his fear. "I worry Eliot might never be held accountable for his crimes by virtue of being a member of your powerful family."

George had a sinking feeling he was right.

When they finally arrived, Nelthorpe told them the Earl had instructed him to bar the policemen from entering the house.

"Let me talk to my parents," George told the impatient policeman.

Allowed entry by the butler, he found his mother and father in the foyer, along with his Uncle Clarence.

"We're not going to permit them to take Eliot away," his mother said.

"You are aware he tried to kill Jane," George retorted.

"Nonsense," his uncle insisted. "Who told you that?"

"I was there. He bound and gagged her and left her in a stall to be trampled by a carthorse."

"That's not his version," his father replied. "He was simply trying to delay things."

George filled his lungs. Losing his temper would achieve nothing. "What about Richard Sharp?"

His mother lifted her chin. "How was I to know Eliot would defend me when I told him Sharp was threatening me? I couldn't depend on you. You were fond of Sharp."

George stared at his mother, wondering how much she suspected about his relationship with Richard. "Eliot killed a man and you think it's all right?"

"It was an accident," his uncle said. "They argued and Sharp fell into the mash tun."

George couldn't allow this foolishness to continue. "I

suppose that explains how the back of his head was caved in with a hammer."

His father shook his head. "All this is moot, Burnley. You must understand that we cannot be a party to Eliot's arrest. I'm sure you don't want to inherit an earldom tainted by scandal. We've made arrangements for Clarence to escort our son to the West Indies."

Jacob was distraught. Jane hadn't made a sound since she stopped sobbing. Cooing soothing endearments, he sat in his late grandmother's rocking chair and cradled his beloved to his chest.

"You have such a lovely voice," she said suddenly.

Not sure what to make of the remark, he stopped carefully picking bits of straw from her hair and glanced down. Her eyes were still closed. Was she asleep or in a state of shock?

"I can't carry a tune," she whispered after a few minutes. "Hopeless at it. Mama says no man will ever want to marry me because I can't hit the right notes."

Tempted to laugh out loud at such a ridiculous notion, he nevertheless controlled the impulse and tightened his arms around her. "I'd marry you if you were the worst singer in Christendom."

She opened her eyes and smiled at him. "You're so good to me, Jacob," she slurred, nose wrinkled as she struggled to sit up. "I stink of horse dung. Let's bathe."

Jacob could think of no better way to soothe her hurts. "Banks," he yelled. "Get Mrs. Banks to run a bath, if you please."

He carried her upstairs and placed her gently on his bed. "May I?" he asked, reaching for the edges of the ruined bodice.

"Mmm," she murmured, her eyes still closed.

She was like a rag doll, so it took some doing to get her undressed. Swallowing hard at the sight of her naked beauty, he wondered if he was doing the right thing. She might regret the impulse to bathe once...

"Sod it," he said to himself. "I'll make sure she doesn't regret it."

Having checked the temperature of the water, he shooed Mrs. Banks out of the boudoir. She probably knew what he planned, but said nothing.

He undressed then lifted Jane from the bed, stepped into the tub and nestled her between his legs. "Come back to me, my love," he whispered.

"Mmm," Jane crooned. "Hot water. Lovely."

She wasn't certain where she was, but the memory of the horror in the stable was fading.

"Feel better?"

Jacob? She might have known Jacob would think to run a bath for her.

Slowly, she opened her eyes, startled to find herself naked in Jacob's arms. She briefly thought to protest, but the solid strength of his chiseled chest at her back distracted her. "You found me in time," she said, as the awful memories returned.

"I did," he replied. "Even though you can't sing."

"What?"

"You mentioned you can't carry a tune."

She giggled. "I must have been delirious."

"And now? Are you still feeling poorly?"

She felt his hard maleness prodding her bottom. "No. I'm feeling amorous, and I see you are too."

"Naughty girl," he growled. "Relax and let me play."

Safe in Jacob's strong arms, she slipped into a euphoric haze as he teased her nipples.

JANE's throaty moans alerted Jacob to the moment she needed more than nipple play and it was perhaps too soon to suggest she touch herself. Truth be told, his swollen cock was also demanding more.

She startled when he lifted her and strode out of the tub with her in his arms.

"Hush," he crooned, as he carried her into his bedroom.

"I'm all wet," she countered when he placed her on his bed.

"Wet is good," he replied, suckling a pert nipple.

"You're right," she agreed, tracing a finger through the rivulets of water on his chest. Then, she reached for his cock, looked into his eyes and whispered, "I want you inside me."

His resolve crumbled, but he had to lessen the pain of her first penetration. "Let me make you ready," he said.

He rubbed his nose in the damp curls at her mons before feasting on the sweet juices. It took only a few flicks of his tongue to bring her to rapture. He silenced her screams with his kiss as he thrust inside her wet heat.

He felt her maidenhead tear, but she clung to him and matched him stroke for stroke. The blissful tightness of her virgin's sheath deafened him to the insistent little voice that kept reminding him to withdraw.

It was only when his seed was about to erupt that he came to his senses and spilled on her belly.

Panting, he collapsed on top of her, his energy drained.

Gradually, he became aware that Jane was twirling her fingers in the sweat on his back—and she was singing!

Jacob is my darling, my darling, my darling, Jacob is my darling, my young cavalier.

The song was centuries out of date and completely off key, but his happy heart and loins didn't give a damn.

WHEN JANE CONSIDERED the noblemen of her acquaintance to whom she might one day have been betrothed, it struck her how fortunate she was to have met Jacob. She'd long been convinced she would surrender her virginity to her husband, but she felt no guilt at giving herself to Jacob. He'd promised she would come virgin to their marriage bed, but in her mind and his, this *was* their marriage bed. Jacob was her destiny. She'd never been more certain of anything in her life.

The thought of another man's mouth on the most intimate part of her body made her shudder. Yet she longed for Jacob to taste her again, and again. The sensations were—indescribable. Wicked, yet not. A delicious, intimate secret she shared only with Jacob.

There'd been fleeting pain, but it paled in comparison to the heady sensation of being one with the man she loved, of giving herself over to the force of his need. She was smugly confident Jacob kept careful control of his emotions. Only with her did he free himself from the restraints necessary for success in a competitive world. She swore a silent oath that she would always be the supportive partner he needed.

Chapter 35

Concessions

Pacing Glenairlie's foyer, George struggled to find a way out of this impasse. His father was correct—he had no wish to inherit an earldom tainted by scandal. It was ironic that he'd long feared his own sexual proclivities would be the cause of scandal. Instead, the actions of a half-brother whose existence he'd barely acknowledged threatened to undermine the very foundations of the earldom.

Suddenly, the way forward struck him. He hurried to the study that would one day be his. "If I'm to overlook Eliot's escape," he told his parents. "I want something in return."

"Such as?" his haughty mother asked.

"Two things."

"Name them," his father insisted gruffly.

"First, I am going to confide a personal secret about myself, and I want your word of honor there'll be no recriminations."

"You mean to tell us that you prefer the affections of men," his mother replied. "We've known it for a while. You neverthe less will make a fine earl. What's the second thing?"

Flabbergasted, George struggled to collect his scattered

thoughts. "You will permit Jane to marry Jacob Longworth, because I plan to name her firstborn son as my heir."

"Absolutely not," his mother replied.

"Agreed," the twin brothers chimed at once, overruling the Countess.

"Very well. I'll throw the policemen off the scent, but only for a short time while you spirit Eliot away."

His uncle marched off immediately, and George made his way to the front door, leaving his mother to take her anger out on her husband.

"Why don't we simply break down the front door?" Walsh asked for the tenth time.

"Because it's more than my job's worth, and yours," Marcus replied. "I'm just as irritated by the incredible disregard for the law as you are, but we have to wait."

"On the bloody doorstep," Walsh huffed. "I'm surprised they didn't send us round to the tradesmen's entrance."

That might have been a quicker way to gain access to the house, but Marcus couldn't admit as much to Walsh.

They stepped back when the door finally opened and Viscount Burnley joined them.

"Well?" Walsh asked rudely.

Burnley pointedly ignored him and directed his reply to Marcus. "I'm afraid Eliot has flown the coop. He's on his way to Liverpool with Uncle Clarence."

"Liverpool?" Walsh queried.

"The docks," Marcus guessed. "Bound for the tropics, unless I am mistaken"

"Probably," George muttered. "We might still be in time to stop them."

Yate and Walsh both hurried to Longworth's carriage, but Marcus hesitated. A little voice told him all wasn't as it seemed. He'd learned over the years to pay attention to that voice. However, there wasn't much he could do about it in the present circumstance, so he joined the other men in the carriage and away they went on what he suspected was a wild goose chase.

Jacob supposed he should be worried about the amount of time that had passed since Yate and the policeman had taken off in his carriage. There were matters to take care of at the brewery. However, he was confident Jenkinson would manage in his absence, and he had no intention of leaving Jane alone.

They'd lain abed, dozing skin to skin for a good while after making love, then they'd dressed and gone down to the drawing room, where they cuddled on the settee. Mrs. Banks served them cocoa.

"This is a grand house," Jane murmured languidly as she sipped her beverage.

"It's been in my family for three generations. My grandfather built it. He was one of the pioneering mill owners of the cotton industry here—personal friend of Samuel Crompton who invented the spinning mule."

"But you haven't carried on his legacy in the cotton industry."

"No. My older brother took on that role. He and I never got along. I wanted to start an enterprise of my own."

"I admire you for it."

"Well, the beer industry has its challenges, but we're making a decent profit. Things look rosier now I don't have the threat of extortion hanging over my head."

"But the vowels."

He realized he hadn't told her. "Sharp lied about buying the IOUs. The original lenders still hold the notes and intend to honor our agreement."

"So, why did Eliot feel the need to hide them?"

"He mustn't have known."

She turned in his arms and kissed his cheek. "I pity him but I'm so relieved for you."

"Your parents can no longer object to our marriage."

"Speaking of my parents," she replied. "They will try to protect Eliot."

Jacob was about to protest when Banks announced the arrival of Viscount Burnley.

JANE RELUCTANTLY LEFT the reassuring comfort of Jacob's embrace and rushed to hug her brother when he entered the drawing room. "Have they arrested Eliot?" she asked.

"No."

Something in his voice gave her pause. "You sound doubtful."

"You're going to have to accept that he may never be caught."

Jacob had risen from the settee. "That's unacceptable," he growled, putting an arm around her waist.

"What are you not telling us?" Jane asked.

"Halliwell intended to set off for the Liverpool docks, believing Eliot was headed there in order to board ship for the West Indies."

"I think I should sit down," Jane replied, sensing she wouldn't like what came next.

Jacob sat next to her and put his arm around her shoulders. "Who told them he was bound for Liverpool?" he asked George.

"I did."

Again, Jane felt uncomfortable with his answer. "But that wasn't true, was it?"

"No. Uncle Clarence is taking him to the Bristol docks. He has a ship there that's due to depart for Jamaica in a day or two."

"So, there's still time to apprehend him," Jacob declared.

Jane was beginning to understand. "You say Halliwell *intended* to go to Liverpool."

George nodded. "It seems he was forbidden to do so by his superintendent. Something to do with jurisdiction."

"But surely..." Jacob began.

"Don't you see, my love," Jane said. "The family has closed ranks."

"Even you, George?" Jacob asked belligerently.

"I agreed to facilitate our half-brother's escape from British justice, although from what I've heard, the heat in Jamaica can be hellishly unbearable, and he'll never be able to return to England."

"That's not funny," Jacob declared. "How could you let him escape after what he did to Jane?"

"I exacted a few sworn promises in return that I felt were more important than seeing our brother swing at the end of a rope."

"Such as?"

"Permission is granted for you and Longworth to marry."

Jane swiveled in Jacob's embrace, elated by the gleam of joy in his eyes. "We can wed," she said hoarsely.

"I, on the other hand, will never marry, for reasons known only to Jane and, it seems, to our parents. So, I plan to name my sister's firstborn son as my heir."

Jacob broke off Jane's ardent kiss. "You mean my son will succeed you as Earl of Leyland?"

"Indeed, if you approve."

Jacob stood and offered his hand to George. "Of course, I approve."

As the two men she loved most in the world shook hands and shared a hearty embrace, Jane reflected on the unexpected twists and turns life sometimes took. She was destined to marry a commoner, but her son would become an earl. Her beloved brother would inherit an earldom free of scandal despite his sexual proclivities. Eliot would live the rest of his life in exile, a fate that would break his mother's heart. And what of Frederick, abandoned by his father in favor of a half-brother he'd known nothing about until recently?

Chapter 36

A Lucky Man

"There's really nothing we can do," Superintendent Findley told Marcus and his constable. "Jamaica is far beyond our reach, I'm afraid."

Marcus had expected as much, but his failure to apprehend a murderer still rankled.

"Surely, sir, we can charge several members of the Yate family with interfering with the course of justice," Walsh declared. "They deliberately aided the killer's escape."

The superintendent glanced at Marcus. "Your young constable has a lot to learn, Halliwell."

Glowering, Walsh made no effort to hide his disgust.

"Yes, sir," Marcus replied.

"That will be all, gentlemen."

"One more thing, if I may, sir," Marcus said, aware what he had to say might annoy his superior officer.

"I said the case is closed."

"Yes, I understand. Since it is closed, I wish to request time off to get married."

"Married?" the superintendent exclaimed. "The confirmed bachelor is getting married?"

Marcus supposed it was out of the ordinary for a man his age to marry, but he didn't appreciate the superintendent's wide-eyed sarcasm. "I'd like two weeks, sir."

"Two weeks!"

"My bride wishes to visit her family in Scotland."

"Granted, I suppose. Without pay, of course."

Though Marcus thought the decision mean-spirited, he was about to acquiesce when Walsh spoke up. "That hardly seems fair, sir. Inspector Halliwell has served this police force for ten years without ever taking time off."

Marcus was astonished and feared Walsh might be summarily dismissed, but he appreciated his assistant's surprising, if ill-advised intervention.

Muttering under his breath, the superintendent raised an eyebrow. "You make a good point," he suddenly replied. "Take three weeks with half pay."

Walsh opened his mouth, probably to object, but Marcus hustled his constable out of the office before their superior officer changed his mind.

As she prepared to walk down the aisle of the Wesleyan Methodist Chapel on Grecian Crescent, Florence took a moment to scan the interior for the first time. A lifelong Presbyterian, she hadn't known what to expect, but the chapel's decor seemed invitingly simple and devoid of statuary. The pews weren't full, but she picked out the bobbing heads of the Yate boys. The Earl and Countess weren't present, but she hadn't expected them to attend.

And there, before the altar, stood the smiling man she loved. They'd both waited a long time to find each other.

"Ready?" George Yate asked as he offered his arm.

Florence inhaled deeply and exchanged a grateful smile with Lady Jane. She'd wager few brides of her social standing could boast of being given away by a viscount and attended by the daughter of an earl. "More than ready, my lord."

"Before we go," the Viscount said. "Jane and I want to thank you for the part you played in raising us."

"You've been more of a mother to me than the Countess," Jane added, as she draped the veil over Florence's face.

"Ye'll make me cry," she sniffled, elated they appreciated how much she loved them.

The Viscount patted her hand. "And Halliwell had better take good care of you, or he'll have me to answer to."

"He will," she replied, aware of how lucky she was to have captured the heart of an honorable man like Marcus Halliwell.

To the dulcet notes of the organ, they began the slow, dignified walk down the aisle.

As HE WATCHED his lovely bride walk toward him, Marcus's heart filled with peaceful joy. Beside him, Walsh fidgeted. Not for the first time, Marcus wondered if asking the constable to act as his best man had been a wise decision. However, it was too late to do anything about it now, and Walsh hadn't stopped telling Marcus how honored he was to be chosen.

He and Eliza had attended this particular church before her death. He felt her presence now, and knew she was content to let him go.

He accepted Florence's warm hand from the Viscount, still annoyed at the part the nobleman had played in helping Eliot Yate escape justice. However, Florence had been honored and pleased by the Viscount's offer to give her away, so Marcus had agreed. After all, his Presbyterian bride had acquiesced to a Methodist wedding.

As he and Florence pledged themselves to each other, a peaceful certainty stole over him. Despite the difficulties he sometimes faced in his job, he derived a great deal of satisfaction from solving murders. Unlike many in the force, he loved being a policeman, and he loved the woman he was marrying. He and his bride had shared intimate touches in the course of their courtship, but his Scottish spitfire had made it clear she was as anxious as he to consummate the marriage.

He was a lucky man indeed.

Upon arrival in Edinburgh, Florence was saddened but not surprised to learn of the deaths of both her parents. The one brother who still lived in the family homestead with his wife and children welcomed them with open arms, enthralled by the news she'd married a policeman. They stayed up late reminiscing by the fire, surrounded by a half-dozen yawning nieces and nephews.

They were tired once they finally retired but a fit of the giggles seized Florence. She supposed the week-long journey from Lancashire to Edinburgh had thrown her off balance, though she and Marcus had taken full advantage of the nights spent at posh inns he assured her he could well afford. They had purchased a bigger bed for their flat in Bolton, but her brother's spare bedroom in the tiny house in Edinburgh boasted no such luxury. Marcus wasn't a small man, and for some inexplicable reason, she found the sight of his big feet protruding from the end of the bed hilariously funny.

"It's not funny," Marcus groused.

"Aye, 'tis," she whispered, climbing on top of him. "Mayhap

if I dinna teck up so much space, ye willna be so uncomfortable."

"Much better," he agreed, when her body molded to his.

"Aye," she agreed, as they began the slow, necessarily silent, journey to rapture.

MARCUS WOULD NEVER ADMIT to Florence that he was glad to be leaving Edinburgh after a week's stay with her family, although she'd likely be the first to agree the bed wasn't comfortable. Still, they'd made the best of it!

Marcus had long since abandoned the notion of ever being a happily married man, yet that's exactly what he was. However, he itched to be back in Bolton doing what he did best. Three weeks away from his job had been more than enough. He wondered what Walsh had been up to in his absence, and if anyone else had been murdered.

Chapter 37

Cracks

Looking up at Holy Trinity's high altar, Jacob turned to Roger Sandiford. "I envy Halliwell his uncomplicated wedding," he murmured. "All this pomp is too much."

His best man shrugged. "If a man marries the daughter of an earl, he has to expect this fuss. I actually have fond memories of marrying Bea in this church."

"I suppose," Jacob replied, thankful for the reminder of what this day was about. Lady Jane Yate would soon be his wife. For her sake, he could tolerate the trumpeted fanfares, the massed choir, the string quartet, the military honor guard, the Yate coat of arms on display throughout the church. There was, of course, no corresponding Longworth coat of arms, an omission that surely wasn't lost on the hundreds of noblemen and women from all over the county that the Earl had insisted on inviting.

It was of some consolation that Jane's disdain for all this nonsense rivaled his own, though he hoped she wouldn't become resentful of the judgmental muttering already audible in the church.

He could almost feel the anger and resentment radiating off the Countess seated in the front pew.

As he turned to welcome his bride, the sight of Jane's stunning beauty robbed him of breath and banished any reservations about his new in-laws. He had to admire her resilience. She'd insisted there was nothing ambiguous about supporting Jacob in his brewery and continuing to lead the local Temperance League. Perhaps she was right that times were changing.

Even her father seemed resigned to accept him as a son-in-law, though people might not think so if they saw the stern set of the Earl's jaw as he escorted Jane down the aisle. His demeanor softened a little when Jane pecked a kiss on his cheek.

Then Jane's warm hand gripped Jacob's and her smile assured him everything would be all right.

JANE HADN'T TOLD Jacob that her father had cajoled the Bishop of Salford into officiating at her wedding. Her fiancé had become increasingly impatient with all the fuss that was part and parcel of a society wedding. The bishop had christened her many moons ago, so she agreed with her parents that his presence was appropriate. She'd never admit as much to Jacob, but she considered all the pomp and circumstance as her due. She was, after all, the daughter of an earl. The fanfare, the massed choir, the military honor guard, the string quartet, the presence of the entire titled aristocracy of Lancashire, the ridiculously long train of her wedding gown, and the myriad of little girls to carry it—all were poignant reminders that it was of no consequence that she was marrying a commoner. The ubiquitous Yate shields were a bit much, but she couldn't blame her father for the ostentatious display of pride in a family that had skirted disaster.

There'd been no news of Uncle Clarence and Eliot, but Frederick had accepted the wedding invitation and sent a magnificent congratulatory bouquet. He'd been assigned a seat with George and her other brothers in one of the front pews. She hoped he would become a sensible member of the family and not turn out to be as devious and troublesome as his half-brother. Not that Francis, Albert, Edward, and Victor were what one might call sensible. Speaking of half-brothers, who would have expected George and Caldwell to develop a friendship?

As the bishop settled into the second quarter hour of his sermon after the vows, Jane's gaze met Jacob's. She would never forget the love in his eyes as he'd repeated his promises, and hoped he heard the same sincerity in her voice. "I love you," she mouthed.

"Love you too," he echoed, twirling his thumb in her palm.

It was a titillating reminder of the sensual delights to come.

Jacob agreed that the wedding banquet should be held at Glenairlie. His own home was grand enough, but he certainly didn't have the staff nor the talented kitchen personnel to cater to such a large crowd. "I fear my jaw is locked in a perpetual smile," he confided to Jane during a lull in the receiving line. "And I've never shaken so many hands."

"Me too," she replied close to his ear. "Remember, you're the curiosity of the day. Our guests are anxious to meet the brewer who captured the heart of an earl's daughter."

He peered down the long hallway. "The lineup seems never-ending."

"My mother had invitations sent to every stately home in the northern counties."

Jacob wasn't certain he should bring up the subject of Eliot, but the topic had to be broached sooner or later. He approached it in a roundabout way. "She seems to be bearing up."

Jane didn't smile. "She's always been good at presenting a brave face to the world—her upbringing as the daughter of a duke, I suppose."

Jacob and his late mother had always gotten along famously and he missed her. She'd have been proud to see him happily wed—to a noblewoman no less. He pitied Jane's poor relationship with her mother, but this wasn't the day to voice those concerns.

"Here comes a couple we can be ourselves with," Jane whispered.

"Halliwell," Jacob exclaimed, shaking the policeman's hand. "And Mrs. Halliwell."

"How was Scotland?" Jane asked her former maid.

"Grand," Florence replied. "'Twas wonderful to see ma family, but we're both glad to be back."

"Indeed," the inspector confirmed. "More rain in Edinburgh than here in Lancashire, and that's saying something."

"Thanks for inviting us," Florence whispered to Jane. "I'm certain 'twas yer doin'. I canna imagine the Countess is thrilled to see us here."

"Well, we're delighted you've come," Jacob replied sincerely.

THE HUNDREDS of guests who sat down to enjoy the lavish wedding banquet heaped praise on the quality and quantity of the dishes and wines. Jane's parents were the perfect hosts. Breeding demanded no less. Her brothers were the life and soul of the party, proposing toast after toast to the happy couple and hinting at shenanigans they had planned for "later."

To the casual observer, it probably seemed as though all was well with the Yate family, but Jane sensed the undercurrents. The Halliwells were possibly the only other people in the ballroom conscious of the cracks in the facade. Eliot's crime had splintered the family.

Only George seemed genuinely happy. Jane was glad he'd forged the future he wanted for himself and the earldom.

Jane's father eventually proposed a toast to his daughter's happiness, but it was brief. She understood that he was too proud to wear his heart on his sleeve in public.

As the dessert was being served, she squealed her relief when Jacob scooped her up and declared his intention to get on with the business of being a good husband. They left the ballroom to loud applause and laughter.

Chapter 38

Rapture

"Where are we going?" Jane asked, when Jacob carried her out of Glenairlie's main entrance.

"My house," he replied. "I don't trust those silly brothers of yours."

"Probably with good reason," she agreed.

Clad in his Sunday best, a beaming Henry stood beside the open door of Jacob's carriage.

"Besides," he said, as he lifted her into the vehicle. "I want to make love to my wife in my own bed."

Her ridiculously long train took a while to stuff inside the carriage. They and Henry ended up in fits of laughter before they set off, cocooned in yards of satin.

"You planned this all along," she teased, when he drew her onto his lap.

She was right. He'd instructed Henry to have the carriage ready to depart the Yate mansion. "Are you upset?"

"No, I'm glad to be free of Glenairlie. Too many painful memories."

"We'll create new memories. My family never gave our home a name. Any suggestions?"

"Yes. Kiss me."

Jacob was happy to obey his wife's command. He intended to nibble her lips gently, to go slowly, but Jane responded hungrily, opening without being coaxed and sucking his tongue into her mouth. His cock responded predictably as he plundered her warm mouth.

When they arrived at the Deane house, he was reluctant to pry his mouth from his bride's. He gathered her up—train and all—and carried her past the applauding servants, up the stairs and into his bedroom. Only then did they break apart as momentum carried them both to the bed.

JANE COLLAPSED ONTO HER BACK, giggling like a child. Jacob loomed over her on hands and knees, his eyes bright with desire. "You can't escape, Jane Longworth."

"I don't wish to," she replied, the giggles banished by the need burning in his gaze.

They gazed at each other for long moments, before he loosened the tiara holding the veil in place and eased it off her head. "I love this fire," he breathed, sifting his fingers through her red tresses.

She reached up to run her fingers over the first signs of stubble on his face. "I love everything about you."

Nostrils flaring, he slowly lowered his head to kiss her again. Intoxicated by the taste of the rich, red wine from the banquet, she draped her arms around his neck and surrendered to the pure pleasure of moist, hungry lips and the gentle abrasion of his beard. Their tongues danced playfully. The warmth of his skin heated her body.

He rained kisses the length of her neck, then brushed his

lips across the swell of her breasts. "Let's get rid of these clothes," he rasped. "I want to see my wife."

He backed off the bed, pulling her upright as he stood. She expected to be gathered into his arms, but he quickly shrugged off his coat and waistcoat before yanking the shirt over his head. She gazed at his sculpted beauty, swaying until he put his hands on her upper arms and looked her in the eyes. "I intend to make love to you, Jane, but I'm not a man to take my pleasure and leave my wife wanting. I meant it when I vowed to worship you with my body."

She blinked away welling tears. "I hope to prove worthy of your adoration," she whispered, flattening her palms against his chest.

His growl echoed in her womb. "You will be."

She cupped his face in her hands. "I long to be completely one with you. No withdrawing this time."

"No fear of that."

He smoothed his hands over her satin-covered breasts, looking puzzled. "I'm not an expert with wedding gowns."

The brush of his thumbs over her nipples made her impatient to be free of the elaborate gown. "You can watch me undress, if you wish."

His eyes darkened, but he made no reply as he sat on the edge of the bed, his long fingers curled into the mattress.

She thought to begin with the impractical boots her mother had insisted upon. Hampered by the yards of material, she hopped about on one foot, trying to look sophisticated as she unbuckled the strap.

A grin tugged at the corners of Jacob's mouth.

"I'm not good at this," she admitted, feeling dizzy.

He patted the bed. "Let me help."

He came to his knees on the carpeted floor as she sat and lifted one foot.

She'd never considered the removal of footwear a sensuous act, but it quickly became arousing as Jacob lingered over unfastening the straps and slowly slipping off each boot. She groaned with pleasure when he kneaded his thumbs into the soles of her feet.

"Shall I help with the hose?" he offered, his hands already halfway up her thighs.

The muscles in a very private place pulsed of their own accord as he rolled the garters down her legs, then the stockings. When he kissed her toes, she whimpered and reached for his broad shoulders.

But he shook his head and sat back on the bed. "You promised I could watch."

Her heart sang at the prospect of a future with a man who liked to tease. Was she brave enough to tease him back?

She stood and turned her back to him. "I don't care if you have to tear it, get this frock off me."

He made an effort to deal with the dozen tiny pearl buttons, then took her at her word and tore the back of the garment open. Buttons popped.

Pretending to be coy, she turned to face him, holding the loosened bodice to her breasts. "I want you, Jacob," she murmured, fluttering her eyelashes.

The arch of his eyebrows indicated he knew she was toying with him, but he rose to the challenge, easing the fabric bit by bit over her breasts and down over her hips until she was free of the gown. He helped her step over the mounds of fabric. "Temptress," he whispered, swirling his tongue over a nipple straining against the silk chemise beneath the dress.

She closed her eyes for a moment, basking in the sensations rippling through her body as she waited for him to remove the chemise.

Suddenly, her arms were in the air and the garment was in Jacob's hands. "Oh," she exclaimed.

"You're more beautiful each time I see you," he rasped, taking her into his embrace, "but you're shivering."

"Warm me," she replied, melting with relief.

"I have just the thing to warm you," he said, holding her hand to his arousal.

She moved her fingers on him, but he lifted her onto the bed. "All in good time," he whispered. "First, I want to feast."

JACOB TOYED BRIEFLY with the notion of removing his trousers, but the garment was the last obstacle remaining between his rampant shaft and Jane's warm sheath. He intended to give them both as much pleasure as possible before his cock had its way.

He raked his eyes over her perfection.

She frowned when he put his arms around her calves and pulled her to the edge of the mattress.

"We'll do nothing against your will," he promised as he knelt, hoping his aching shaft was paying attention now that he had set eyes on the pink folds of Jane's most intimate place. He risked mentioning his thirst to taste her essence. "I crave your mouth there—again," she'd whispered. Elated, he parted her nether lips with his thumbs before bending his head to suckle.

Her honeyed juices filled his senses. The whimpering sounds that emerged from her throat echoed in his sac. He flicked his tongue over the proud pearl, contentedly certain she was nearing a pinnacle as the mewling became more frenzied.

He tightened his hold on her legs when she screamed loud and long, arching off the bed, the linens clutched in her fisted hands. Watching her savor the euphoria of her release almost brought him to tears. It was the most beautiful sight he had ever seen.

JANE SLOWLY DRIFTED BACK to earth and opened her eyes. Jacob had lifted her to previously unknown heights of ecstasy, but there was yet something she craved. "Fill me," she whispered, awed by the love in his gaze—and the thickness of the proud lance jutting from his body. While she'd been soaring on clouds, he'd evidently removed his trousers and now knelt between her legs.

"I screamed," she murmured.

"Yes," he said with a smile, "I loved it." He lifted her hips. "Put your legs around me. I want to bury myself deep inside you. Ready?"

She nodded as he positioned the swollen tip of his manhood at her opening. Perhaps it was because she was more relaxed this time that there was no pain. Instead, exquisite sensations blossomed as he slowly penetrated, then withdrew, then went deeper. "Jacob," she breathed, as every slow thrust carried her closer and closer to another crescendo.

His body heated. They fell into a faster rhythm, matching each other stroke for stroke, growl for growl. She recognized the signs of his impending release. She and Jacob were locked in a journey to ecstasy that would bond them forever.

"Come with me," he exclaimed, as his seed bathed her womb. She teetered on the edge of something monumental. She was falling...falling, but he held her fast as she tumbled into rapture.

Chapter 39

The Bull By The Horns

Jenkinson had jovially convinced Jacob they could manage without him at the brewery, so the newlyweds had spent most of the week after the wedding in bed, learning how to please each other. He'd sensed from their first meeting that Jane was a woman capable of great passion, and his intuition had been borne out. He'd never dreamt he would find a woman who'd bring him such sexual satisfaction. Come to think on it, *satisfaction* was a totally inadequate word for the rapturous heights Jane brought him to.

His servants were elated he'd married well, and according to Mrs. Banks, they apparently boasted to anyone who would listen that their master had married a lady.

However, there'd been no word from Jane's family. She hadn't commented on their silence, but Jacob sensed it bothered her.

His suspicions were confirmed when they finally received an invitation to dine at Glenairlie. Jane couldn't conceal her relief. "At last," she exclaimed. "I knew my parents would come around. It's going to be all right."

"I hope I use the right knife and fork," he quipped, as they boarded their carriage on the evening of the dinner.

"You don't fool me," his wife replied. "You're an educated man who probably knows more about table manners than all my brothers combined, with the exception of George, of course."

The knot in his belly eased. He'd been apprehensive about this first social encounter with his in-laws, but Jane's obvious pride in him banished his fears. "Of course," he echoed.

When they arrived at Glenairlie, Nelthorpe's enthusiastic greeting reinforced his confidence. "I don't think I've seen the man smile before," he whispered to Jane as they followed the dignified butler to the drawing room.

"Behave," she teased with a smile.

"Where's the fun in that?" he retorted.

"Longworth, my boy," the Earl gushed, extending his hand. "Good to see you."

"My lord," Jacob replied, accepting the handshake.

The Viscount clapped a hand on his shoulder. "Your son-in-law's name is Jacob, Papa," he told his father.

"Quite so," the Earl replied.

Jacob took no offense. He'd secured the prize. He hoped the Earl would eventually come down from his ivory tower, mainly for Jane's sake. He would never be able to refer to the Earl as his *Papa*. Only one man had earned that title, and Jeremiah Longworth had passed on.

The Countess nodded an icy greeting.

Jane's brothers shook his hand enthusiastically. He was confident he had allies who must be as shaken as Jane by what they'd learned about their parents and half-brothers.

The conversation was lively, the Earl asking many insightful questions about the brewing industry. Jacob got the feeling he was being tested, but Jane's smile reassured him that he'd impressed her father.

The Earl escorted Jane into dinner, and Jacob was informed he was to be the Countess's escort. He wished his parents were still alive to see him escort a haughty noblewoman into dinner. She remained silent throughout the meal. He realized sadly that she would always disdain commoners. It was nothing personal against him. He pitied the woman who couldn't bring herself to enjoy her only daughter's happiness. Jane sparkled, clearly happy to be back with her family. He was proud and humbled that this beautiful, charismatic woman was his loving wife.

After dinner, the ladies retired to the drawing room while the men enjoyed a glass of brandy. The Viscount and the Earl smoked cigars. Jacob politely declined.

"So, Longworth," the Earl declared. "I trust you've talked Jane out of this Temperance nonsense."

Jacob had a choice. He could pander to his father-in-law's vanity or he could say things Jane would never have the courage to say to her father. A faint lingering trace of Jane's lavender perfume spurred him on. "Do you know why she joined the Temperance League, my lord?"

The Earl leaned back and blew an impressive smoke ring. "Some foolish feminine fancy, I suppose."

"Actually, Sir, she joined in the hopes you and Lord Francis might take the notion of moderation to heart. She fears you both imbibe too much alcohol."

George Yate laughed out loud.

"I say," Francis spluttered. "Steady on."

The Earl stared at his son-in-law for long moments before the trace of a smile tugged at his lips. "I admire a man who's not afraid to take the bull by the horns," he said. "You'll do, Jacob."

Relieved to return to the dining room after a stilted thirty-minute conversation with her mother, Jane noticed a subtle change in her father's demeanor toward Jacob. She waited until they were on their way home in the carriage before mentioning it to her husband. "What on earth did you say to Papa in my absence?" she asked.

"Nothing," he replied. "How was your mother?"

"Grieving," she said. "She probably blames me for Eliot's fate. But don't change the subject."

"Why would she blame you?"

"You're not going to tell me, are you?"

"No. Suffice it to say, I think your father now accepts me."

Jane decided to leave it at that. After all, she could always ask George.

Chapter 40

Dinosaur

Considering a murderer had escaped more or less scot-free, Marcus thought the meeting with the superintendent went reasonably well. Findley seemed to think the most significant outcome of the case was that Marcus and Walsh had avoided upsetting the aristocratic Yate family. Marcus sensed his constable's seething tension, but Walsh kept control of his anger.

"I'm still puzzled as to how Lord Albert's IOU came to be in the Earl's desk," their superior said.

"We surmise Eliot Yate took it from Sharp, and either he or Lord Clarence planted it there," Walsh replied.

Marcus was pleased with Walsh's explanation but felt more could be added. "The former planned to see his twin hanged for the murder and then claim the title for himself."

"And the boy wanted to divert suspicion away from himself," Walsh said. "We think he must have known at that point that the Earl wasn't his father, so perhaps he was motivated by anger."

"Or Lord Clarence suggested it."

"And what about the extortion letter sent to the brewer?" Findley asked.

Marcus had thought long and hard on this very topic. "My theory is that the main purpose of that letter wasn't extortion. The writer couldn't know Sharp had lied about buying the IOUs. It was to warn Longworth off pursuing Lady Jane. Clarence, and perhaps his son, couldn't abide the idea of a commoner marrying into the family."

"In other words," Walsh continued. "Murder and extortion were considered fine by the Yates, but diluting the bloodline was beyond the pale."

Findley narrowed his eyes, clearly not certain what to make of the constable's remark. They were gruffly dismissed with a wave of the hand.

"You should be careful," Marcus told Walsh when they reached the outdoors. "Our superiors don't promote men who rock the boat."

Walsh shrugged. "That may have been true in your day. Times are changing, old chap."

Marcus bristled. "I may be a dinosaur, young man," he replied. "But I can still teach you a thing or two."

"I'm counting on it, sir," Walsh replied with a cryptic smile.

Chapter 41

New Hope

George and Jacob stood when Jane returned to the drawing room after sitting beside her father's sickbed.

"Any improvement?" her husband asked, as the men regained their seats.

Jane shook her head. "He's given up," she replied, nigh on choking on the words when her brother paled. "Incredibly enough, he misses Mama."

"It's ironic," George said softly. "Her bastard's crime and punishment killed her, now it's about to take Papa, a scant three months after she died of a broken heart."

"Well, at least you're about to inherit an earldom free of scandal," Jacob said. "Which is what your parents wanted."

"Another irony, since I seemingly did all I could to risk the earldom's reputation."

Jane hated the guilt in her brother's voice and sought to alleviate the mood. "I was able to give Papa some good news," she teased, smiling at Jacob who already knew the secret.

"Good news?" George replied half-heartedly.

"My wife is carrying your heir," Jacob announced.

Jane glared. "I wanted to tell him."

"Sorry, I couldn't resist."

George stared at Jane. "You're with child? Already?"

Jacob frowned. "What's that supposed to mean? We are married, you know."

"Absolutely nothing," George replied, as he launched at Jane and twirled her around. "Forgive me. I'm just so delighted for you both."

"Funnily enough," Jane panted. "That's exactly what Papa asked when I told him."

She paused, not sure if she should divulge what her father had confided.

"Imagine," George exclaimed. "The man sired six children, and he has the nerve to say that to you."

"I think he was just surprised," Jane replied, deciding George should hear what else their father had said. "He told me he can die content, now he knows you have an heir on the way who's related to you by blood."

George slumped into an armchair, put his head in his hands, and wept.

IT HAD TAKEN A WHILE, but Florence had gradually been accepted by Jacob Longworth's household staff. After all, it was only to be expected that a woman of quality would require the services of a lady's maid.

Florence realized how lucky she was to still have a good position after her marriage. The tragic events involving Lord Eliot and the death of the Countess would have rendered it impossible to return to Glenairlie.

Life among Mr. Longworth's servants was a new beginning. Her position meant returning home late at night, but Marcus always came to pick her up in a hackney. How she loved that dear man.

She'd actually seen little of her mistress since the Earl had fallen ill. Lady Jane had given her the nights off, since she'd been spending long hours at her father's bedside.

Florence suspected Lady Jane was with child, and she fervently hoped she'd told her dying father the good news.

When the time was right, Florence would share her surprising news with the Longworths. Expecting a child at her age was nerve-wracking, but Marcus was over the moon with joy and insisted all would be well.

Historical Footnotes

COTTON COPS

You may be wondering why I gave this series the title COTTON COPS MYSTERIES. It's a play on the word for a spindle used in the cotton industry (cop), and of course, the slang word for a policeman. http://revealinghistories.org.uk/why-was-cotton-so-important-in-north-west-england/objects/two-cotton-cops.html

BOLTON

I chose Bolton as the setting for this story and the others in the series for one simple reason—I was born and went to school there! https://en.wikipedia.org/wiki/Bolton

You may be aware that I'm an amateur genealogist. Many of my nineteenth-century ancestors worked as spinners in the cotton mills.

LANCASHIRE

The Industrial Revolution changed Lancashire forever. Its damp climate was ideal for the cotton industry. which developed rapidly. Fortunes were made by the *nouveau riche* industrialists. These self-made men became the new "aristocracy," their power based on wealth, and not titles and privilege.

Roger Sandiford, the hero of *The Heart's Choice*, is one such mill owner.

Lancashire was the first industrial society in the world, the place where anything and everything was made and where coal was mined. It was the birthplace of the factory system, and it needed a big population to operate the mines and factories. The first canal in the world was built in Lancashire, with more canals and railways following by the early 1830s. The workforce required was far bigger than the existing Lancashire population and had to be imported from other counties, and from Ireland and Scotland. These men and women came from rural areas to live crammed together in the cities. Villages fast became towns.

Statistics show that Lancashire had a considerable crime rate compared with the rest of the country. In 1836, 2568 Lancastrians were convicted or tried for serious offenses.

Some towns formed their own police forces, but there was a growing demand for a county-wide force modeled on the London Metropolitan Police, brought into existence in 1829 by Sir Robert Peel. https://en.wikipedia.org/wiki/Robert_Peel. The Lancashire Constabulary was formed in 1840. https://en.wikipedia.org/wiki/Lancashire_Constabulary

THE COTTON FAMINE
https://en.wikipedia.org/wiki/Lancashire_Cotton_Famine

BOLTON BOROUGH POLICE
https://en.wikipedia.org/wiki/Bolton_Borough_Police
BTW, my father was present at the disaster mentioned in this article.

POLICING IN THE 19TH CENTURY & POLICE VIOLENCE https://www.amazon.com/Victorian-Policing-Gaynor-Haliday/dp/1526706121

THE LEYLAND HUNDRED is an historic subdivision of the county of Lancashire. https://en.wikipedia.org/wiki/Leyland_Hundred

Also by Anna Markland

Cotton Cops Mystery Series

The Heart's Choice

Music Hall Queen

Trouble Brewing

OTHER SERIES

Montbryce Legacy

Earls are Wild

FitzRam Family Dynasty

Clash of the Tartans

Montbryce Dynasty

The House of Pendray

Viking Roots Medieval

Von Wolfenberg Dynasty

The Caledonia Chronicles

Highland Whisky Kings

The UnDukes

Ruff Wooing

About the Author

Anna is a USA Today bestseller who has authored more than sixty award-winning and much-loved Medieval, Viking, Highlander, Elizabethan, Regency, and Victorian historical romances. No matter the historical or geographic setting, many of her series recount the adventures of successive generations of one family, with emphasis on the importance of ancestry and honor. A detailed list with links can be found at https://www.annamarkland.com/

If you enjoy this book, please consider writing a review. Reviews help other readers find books.

A small press bound by the belief that every voice matters.

Sign up for our newsletter to learn about new releases and more.
https://oliver-heberbooks.com/subscribe/

Follow us on social media:

facebook.com/oliverheberbooks

instagram.com/oliverheberbooks

amazon.com/oliverheberbooks

youtube.com/@OliverHeberBooksPublisher